"Go away."

They weren't exactly words that should make one feel cheerful, Adam thought. Especially given the fact that he had traveled over two thousand miles to hear them.

But he did. He felt cheerful.

It wasn't, he told himself firmly, because he was seeing her again, after a space of nearly seven years.

"I told you to go away," Tory said again, resolutely.

Adam regarded her thoughtfully. If he was not mistaken, that was fire he saw in her eyes.

"I'm not leaving." The words came from his mouth, all right, but they really surprised him. Because he didn't want to be here in the first place. He'd come only because of that letter. In fact, all the way here he had hoped for a reaction like this from her.

And yet he knew without a doubt that this time he couldn't walk away....

Dear Reader,

Silhouette Romance novels aren't just for other women—the wonder of a Silhouette Romance is that it can touch *your* heart. And this month's selections are guaranteed to leave you smiling!

In Suzanne McMinn's engaging BUNDLES OF JOY title, *The Billionaire and the Bassinet*, a blue blood finds his hardened heart irrevocably tamed. This month's FABULOUS FATHERS offering by Jodi O'Donnell features an emotional, heartwarming twist you won't soon forget; in *Dr. Dad to the Rescue*, a man discovers strength and the healing power of love from one *very* special lady. *Marrying O'Malley*, the renegade who'd been her childhood nemesis, seemed the perfect way for a bride-to-be to thwart an unwanted betrothal—until their unlikely alliance stirred an even more incredible passion; don't miss this latest winner by Elizabeth August!

The Cowboy Proposes...Marriage? Get the charming lowdown as WRANGLERS & LACE continues with this sizzling story by Cathy Forsythe. Cara Colter will make you laugh and cry with *A Bride Worth Waiting For*, the story of the boy next door who *didn't* get the girl, but who'll stop at nothing to have her now. For readers who love powerful, dramatic stories, you won't want to miss *Paternity Lessons*, Maris Soule's uplifting FAMILY MATTERS tale.

Enjoy this month's titles—and please drop me a line about *why* you keep coming back to Romance. I want to make sure we continue fulfilling *your* dreams!

Regards,

Mary-Theresa Hussey

Mary-Theresa Hussey
Senior Editor Silhouette Romance

Please address questions and book requests to:
Silhouette Reader Service
U.S.: 3010 Walden Ave., P.O. Box 1325, Buffalo, NY 14269
Canadian: P.O. Box 609, Fort Erie, Ont. L2A 5X3

A BRIDE WORTH WAITING FOR

Cara Colter

Silhouette
ROMANCE™
Published by Silhouette Books
America's Publisher of Contemporary Romance

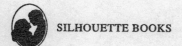

To my sisters,
Anna and Avon,
with love.

SILHOUETTE BOOKS

ISBN 0-373-19388-2

A BRIDE WORTH WAITING FOR

Copyright © 1999 by Cara Colter

This edition published by arrangement with Harlequin Books S.A.

® and TM are trademarks of Harlequin Books S.A., used under license. Trademarks indicated with ® are registered in the United States Patent and Trademark Office, the Canadian Trade Marks Office and in other countries.

Visit us at www.romance.net

Printed in U.S.A.

Books by Cara Colter

Silhouette Romance

Dare To Dream #491
Baby in Blue #1161
Husband in Red #1243
The Cowboy, the Baby and the Bride-to-Be #1319
Truly Daddy #1363
A Bride Worth Waiting For #1388

CARA COLTER

shares ten acres in the wild Kootenay region of British Columbia with the man of her dreams, three children, two horses, a cat with no tail, and a golden retriever who answers best to "bad dog." She loves reading, writing and the woods in winter (no bears). She says life's delights include an automatic garage door opener and the skylight over the bed that allows her to see the stars at night.

She also says, "I have not lived a neat and tidy life, and used to envy those who did. Now I see my struggles as having given me a deep appreciation of life, and of love, that I hope I succeed in passing on through the stories that I tell."

Dear Adam,

I asked my lawyer to wait a year before sending this to you. Tory will need time. She needs to know she can make it on her own.

But she needs to laugh, too.

She was my angel. And now, if things work the way I think they will, I'm going to be hers.

This is my last request, Adam, and only you can fulfill it. I know how much you loved her. Go home. Make her laugh again.

She was always a little afraid of how you grabbed life with both hands. But she knows a little more about life now; she won't be so afraid to take what it offers her.

You were my best friend, besides her. I know why you stayed away. She was mad at you, and probably still is, but I wasn't. I'm watching out for you. I promise.

Mark

Chapter One

"**G**o away."

They weren't exactly words that should make one feel cheerful, Adam thought. Especially given the fact he had traveled over two thousand miles to hear them.

But he did feel cheerful. Probably because this insane mission was over before it had even started.

It wasn't, he told himself firmly, because he was seeing her again, after a space of nearly seven years.

"I told you to go away," she said again, resolutely.

He regarded her thoughtfully. She was on the other side of her screen door, her arms folded over her chest, her foot tapping impatiently, and if he was not mistaken, with fire in her eyes.

She had not been beautiful all those years ago, and she had not matured into beauty.

In fact, she was remarkably unchanged. On the flight here he had picked out women of his age and hers, and studied them. And been reassured. That she would have changed. That she would be plump and frumpy. Or that a smooth veneer of sophistication would have chased away the elfin charm that had made him call her "cute," a description she had always reacted to with chagrin, which only made her cuter.

But she was still cute. Not plump. Certainly not frumpy. No veneer of sophistication. Though he knew her to be his own age, thirty, she looked astoundingly like the first time he had seen her in sixth grade—her baseball cap on backward, that same riot of red-gold curls scattered around her face, those same freckles sprinkled across the bridge of her little snub nose, a pointed chin, little bow lips. Except now there was no baseball cap and that chin was lifted at him in defiance, the bows of her lips faintly downturned in disapproval.

That first time she'd had on a too-big Stampeders jersey, and rolled up jeans that showed a Band-Aid on her knee. She had been smiling, though. A smile so full of mischief and warmth it had melted his twelve-year-old heart in a way it had never been touched before. Or since.

Today she wore a too-large man's shirt over a pair of black bicycle shorts. Silly, but he checked the knees, his eyes drifting over the rest of her on the way down. She'd mourned her boyish build all through adolescence, and as far as he could tell it was unchanged. She was willowy and slender as a young tree.

"I've got about as many curves as a ruler," she used to lament.

By then she was already the ruler of his heart. It had made him blind for all time to the attractions of fuller-figured women.

He found her knees, finally, and peered through the screen.

She tucked one slim leg behind her, but not before he

saw the smudge that struck him, foolishly, as being utterly lovely.

"I was out back in the garden," she said defensively.

"I didn't say anything."

"Anyway, you're leaving." She reached out and snapped the lock on the screen, as if he was some sort of barbarian, who would enter her house without an invitation, barge by her, sit on her sofa and demand tea. No. Beer.

Did she really think of him like that? Of course she did. That was why he'd been overlooked for someone with a better pedigree.

Of course if she *really* thought of him like that, she would know the flimsy screen door, with its fancy heritage scrolling in the corners, wouldn't keep him out. Probably couldn't keep a determined kitten out.

"I'm not leaving." The words came from his mouth, all right, but they really surprised him. Because he didn't want to be here in the first place. All the way here he had hoped and maybe even prayed for a reaction like this from her. So he could turn on his heel and catch the next flight back to Toronto. That would be enough to soothe his conscience. He'd flown all the way here, hadn't he? Who could say he had not tried his hardest? Not made his best effort?

"If you don't go away, I'll call the police."

He wondered if he should tell her the truth. About the letter in his pocket. Something told him the time was not right.

"No you won't," he said. "You won't call the police."

She glared at him. Her eyes were dark brown, shot through with gold. Immense eyes. They had always been her best feature, dancing with the light that was inside of her.

"I have nothing to say to you."

"We could always talk about the dirt on your knees."

She glared at him, tossed her head and slammed the inside door. The beveled glass insert rattled.

Not something a man who had just traveled two thousand one hundred and twenty-five miles should find amusing.

But he did.

It wasn't, he told himself firmly, seeing her again that was causing this sensation inside him—like a light had been turned on in darkness.

He shoved his hands in his pockets, and rocked back on his heels. He turned slowly from her door. She lived only a block or two from where they had grown up together. Her, and him. And Mark.

The community of Sunnyside. A beautiful old part of the city, bordering the banks of the Bow River. From here, on her covered porch, he could look south up her street, and see the park that ran parallel to the river for most of its journey through Calgary. A couple of runners enjoyed the paved path under huge trees.

He noticed she had a swing on her porch, full of plump gray and pink pillows and he went and sat on it. Out of the corner of his eye he saw a curtain twitch angrily into place.

He rocked slowly with one foot. He liked Calgary. He'd been struck by that an hour earlier when the plane circled. That he liked this city. Had missed it.

This neighborhood was changing so rapidly. Young professionals were snapping up the dignified old houses just across the river from the downtown core and doing incredible renovations on them.

That trend had actually started when he and his dad had moved here years ago. He'd been in the sixth grade.

Her father, Tory's, was a doctor, and had owned the beautifully kept old house on one side of his. Mark's parents, a psychologist and a veterinarian, owned an equally beautiful one on the other.

His house, a ramshackle rental, was right in the middle. Him and his dad, a mechanic with grease under his nails, doing their best to make it after the death of his mom.

He heard the window squeak open behind him.

"Get lost!" she snapped.

"No," he said.

The window slammed shut.

He sighed with something like pleasure. Tory in a temper.

Her name was really Victoria. Victoria Bradbury, a good name for a heroine in an old English novel, but a terrible one for a tomboy who climbed trees and had perpetually scuffed knees. And a temper like a skyrocket going off.

He looked around her porch with interest. The house was probably sixty years old or more, well kept, nicely painted—yellow with gray trim. He noticed she had a gift with flowers, just as her mother had had. The window boxes around the porch rioted with color, which was an accomplishment in the first week of June in a city with such a short growing season.

Her house, back then, had always had flowers. And Mark's parents had had beautifully landscaped no-maintenance shrubs and bark mulch. His own yard had sported the hulks of cars.

He supposed that's why he was staying. To show her what he had become. A lawyer now, the shoes he was wearing worth more than his dad used to pay for a month's rent on that old falling down house.

The thing was, he remembered, she had never seemed to care what he had come from.

And neither had Mark.

They had taken him under wing from the very first day he'd moved in. They had become the three musketeers—ridden their bikes up and down these very streets, built tree houses, walked forever along that path by the river. Their doors had always been open to him, both of their mothers treating him like he was one of their families.

He felt the strangest clawing sensation in his throat.

Remembering. Those bright days so full of laughter and kinship.

Love.

That was not too strong a word for what the three of them had shared, for what passed in and out of the doors of those three side-by-side houses.

Of course, the inevitable had happened.

They got older and the love changed. He and Mark had both fallen in love with her.

And she had chosen Mark.

The swing was squeaking outrageously. The sun was sinking and had bathed the street and its gorgeous huge trees and old houses in the most resplendent light.

He took the letter out of his pocket, opened it and began to read it again. For at least the hundredth time.

Tory inched the curtain back, and looked out. He was still there, sitting in her porch swing, seeming not to care that it had grown quite dark out.

And probably cold.

"Don't you dare care if he's cold," she muttered to herself.

Adam.

She had nearly fainted when she had opened the door and he had been standing there.

The same and yet very different, too.

The same since he was so recklessly handsome that it took a person's breath away.

His hair, though shorter now, was black and faintly wavy and still fell over one eye. Obsidian dark, those eyes, glinting with hints of silver laughter, of mischief. A straight nose, a wide sensuous mouth, clean sparkling teeth, that scar was still on his chin from the time he'd split it open riding his bike over a jump neither she nor Mark would try.

He had laughed, devil-may-care, when her mother had insisted on taking him to the hospital for stitches.

The next week he'd broken his arm going over the same jump.

It didn't look like he laughed quite so much these days. The line around his mouth seemed firm and stern, and the light in his eyes, when she had first opened the door, had been distinctly grim. A man with a mission.

When she'd told him to go away, that old familiar glint of humor had lit somewhere at the back of his eyes. And then it had deepened when he had spotted the dirt on her knees.

She shivered involuntarily as she thought of those black eyes drifting down her with easy familiarity, his gaze nearly as powerful, altogether as sensuous, as a touch.

He had always had that in him. Magnetism. A place in him that could not be tamed, his presence electrifying, making other boys seem smaller, infinitely less interesting, as if they were black-and-white cutouts, and he was three dimensional and in living color.

Even Mark.

Tory had always thought Adam would mature to be the kind of man with a wild side. That he would end up in black leather, jumping canyons on those motorcycles he had loved so much as a teenager. Or traveling the world in search of adventure—crocodiles to wrestle, damsels to rescue.

There was nothing ordinary about him, so she had thought he would do extraordinary things. Become a secret agent. Climb Mount Everest. Sail solo around the world. Explore outer space.

When she'd heard he was a lawyer, she couldn't believe it. Had felt disappointed, almost. Adam, a lawyer? It seemed unthinkable.

Until she saw him standing on her porch, oozing self-confidence and wealth. Of course, the self-confidence he had always had in abundance.

But somehow she never would have imagined him in those shoes, the silk shirt with the tie slightly askew, the knife-pressed pants.

She looked out on her porch again. He used to smoke, but somehow she knew he wouldn't anymore.

The wild boy banished.

But still there, lurking in those eyes and that smile.

"Go away," she whispered.

The swing creaked.

He wasn't going away.

She knew he would be a good lawyer. Better than good. He'd always had a talent for reading people. He always knew what they would do. He was so smart that sometimes she and Mark had exchanged awed looks behind his back. And at his core, he had a toughness, that neither she nor Mark had. A toughness that had less to do with being a mechanic's son than his deep certainty of who he was and what kind of treatment he would accept at the hands of the world.

She knew he thought she'd give in and go out there. Lured by old affections or curiosity.

But she wasn't going to give him the satisfaction. Let him sit out there all night.

She went into her bathroom and slammed the door, regarded herself in the mirror with ill humor. She looked like a little kid. And felt like one, too. She reached down and rubbed the dirt off her knee. With spit.

He looked so sophisticated now. She bet he dated lacquered ladies who could wear sequined gowns and look dazzling instead of ridiculous. He probably took them to the opera.

Adam Reed at the opera.

When had he become that kind of guy instead of the boy who took his motorcycle apart in his backyard, looked over his fence into hers, grinning, the black smudge of motor oil across his cheek making him look more wildly appealing than ever?

No boy left in him. All man out there on her doorstep. At least six foot one of it, the adolescent promise of broadness through the chest and shoulders now completely realized. Easy animal strength lingering just below the surface of those well-cut clothes. Oh yes, that wild side still there, glittering dangerously just below the surface of dark eyes, serving to make him mysterious. Intriguing. Dangerously attractive.

Had she reached out and locked her screen door to keep him out, or herself in?

She wondered if he was married. In the mirror she watched the blood drain from her own face making her freckles stand out like random dots from a felt pen. She almost felt like she had taken a bad blow to the stomach.

"Oh, what do you care if he's married?" she chastised herself. She told herself she only cared about the woman. Married to an insensitive cad like him.

But she knew she was lying to herself, and that's why she knew she absolutely had to ignore him until he went away.

She tiptoed out of the bathroom. The house was in darkness now. She looked out the window.

He was still there.

And if there was anything of the old Adam in him he would still be there in the morning. Next week. Next month.

She could not outwait him. She knew that. She had only been able to say no to him once.

Why was she so afraid of him? Let him have his say, and be on his way. She sighed, and went and got an afghan from off the back of her couch. Because of Calgary's proximity to the Rocky Mountains there was almost always a nip in the air at night. Not that Adam had ever seemed to feel it!

"Don't do this," she told herself. But she knew that she would. And she knew he knew she would.

She opened the front door and slipped out into the darkness of her porch.

The swing stilled.

She went and sat beside him, pulling the blanket around her shoulders against the chill in the air, a small but comforting barrier against him.

"You're the most stubborn man I ever met," she said.

He smelled heavenly. Of sunshine and aftershave and cleanliness.

He reached out and unerringly found a hand, her hand, in the folds of the afghan. His hands were surprisingly warm considering how long he had sat out here in the cold.

She ordered herself to pull her hand away. Her mind mutinied.

Instead, she turned and looked at him.

His eyes were dark and full of mystery. And something else as he looked at her.

"It's like time rolling back seeing you all wrapped up in that blanket."

"Like a sausage," she said dourly.

He showed her his teeth, straight and white and strong. "More like the Indian princess in *Peter Pan*. You were always the first one cold."

"Cold hands, warm heart," they said together.

He laughed, but she felt angry with herself, drawn into the past against her will.

"You can't roll back time," she told him, and this time she did snatch her hand away, tucked it safely inside the fold of her blanket, and studied her neighbor's window across the street. New drapes. Horizontal. She decided she hated them.

"I know," he said, and she heard something in his voice that crumpled her defenses. Weariness. Regret.

"You never came," she whispered.

He was silent. And finally, his voice hoarse, he said "I'm sorry."

"He was your best friend, and you never came when he died." She turned and looked him full in the face. It was his turn to look away. "You never came. All the time he was sick."

He didn't apologize again.

"Why are you here now?" she demanded, sorry he was here, sorry she was so bloody glad he was here, sorry for how she had loved the feel of her hand in his.

Sorry for the way the streetlight made his features look so damnably handsome.

"I'm just back for a visit," he said softly. "I hoped we could spend some time together."

"I don't think so," she said stiffly, which, his lawyer's mind noted, was quite different than an out and out no.

"I don't suppose you've ever gone Rollerblading, have you?" Rollerblading, he thought. She's going to think I'm crazy. But he had the agenda memorized and that was item one. He would break the other three—kite flying, a ride on a bicycle built for two, and a trip to Sylvan Lake to watch the stars from lawn chairs—to her later. Once he had his foot in the door.

She was looking at him incredulously, as if he'd lost his mind, which seemed like a distinct possibility. Seeing her under the glow of the streetlight like this, having felt briefly, the soft strength and warmth of her hand in his, he could feel time shifting, pulling him back....

"Are you crazy?" she asked.

"I think so," he answered. Her eyes were different after all, he realized. Back then they had always had a smile in them. Now they looked angry, and a bit sad.

She didn't look like that person who used to laugh so hard she had worried about wetting her pants.

Where did that side of a person go to?

"Look," she said, her voice suddenly hard, "I don't know what you're trying to do, but don't bother. I needed you—Mark needed you—a long time ago. It's too late, now."

She got up in a single flounce, the blanket swinging regally around her, and fixed him with a glare that turned her from Tory to Victoria Bradbury in an instant. "Go back to where you came from. Don't bother me anymore."

He got up too, looked down at her, into her blazing eyes and then at the soft fullness of her lips.

He had kissed those lips. And the sweetness of them had never left him.

He gave himself a mental shake.

She was giving him a way out.

Take it and run.

He had a busy life back in Toronto. He couldn't afford to take a week off right now. He had a gorgeous, classy girlfriend who would say yes in a minute when he got around to asking her to marry him. He wondered now what he'd been waiting for.

"I'll be back tomorrow," he said softly. "Around ten."

And he went off her porch, to her sputtered, "Don't bother."

He knew, just like the big bad wolf, he'd have to come at nine to catch her.

He had taken a cab, but he decided he'd walk back to his hotel, just across the river. He realized as he went, he was whistling.

And that it had been a very long time since he had whistled.

The hotel room was very posh. For a mechanic's son he had adjusted to poshness with complete ease.

He glanced at his watch. Nearly eleven Calgary time, which meant it was close to one in the morning Eastern time. Too late to call Kathleen, and he was glad. He hadn't told her the details of this trip, only that it was business. Which it was. Or had been. Strictly business.

Until he saw Tory.

Now he felt like Kathleen would hear it in his voice.

Hear what in your voice? he asked himself.

The pull of the past. Things that were once certain becoming uncertain.

He'd thought he and Kathleen, also a lawyer, made an excellent couple, and that he was nearly ready to make a commitment to her.

Until the exact moment Tory had opened her door.

And then nothing seemed assured anymore. Kathleen, an ex-model with her raven black hair and sapphire eyes, wavering in his mind like a mirage.

Impatiently, Adam went over to the tiny fridge and investigated the contents. He took a cola even though he knew it would probably chase away sleep until dawn streaked the sky.

When had he become so old and stable that he didn't drink cola at night because it kept him awake?

He had seen a different man reflected back at him through Tory's eyes. She still saw in him the man-child, who had delighted in walking close to the wild side.

In truth, not just the soda would keep him awake tonight. A strange energy seemed to be singing through his veins.

He picked up his briefcase, moved to the table and snapped it open. Neat stacks of legal briefs stared back at him, the work of a man who didn't drink cola at night because it might keep him awake.

Did she know he was a lawyer? She hadn't asked. Would she ask tomorrow? Would she ask him why?

And would he tell her the truth?

He had contemplated his career long and hard before choosing. He had thought about becoming a doctor, just like her old man.

The thought, unfortunately, made him squeamish. He had always been able to hide his squeamish side from Tory and Mark, who seemed to think he was tough in every respect. And in some respects he had been. He had a high threshold for pain. He liked doing things that were thrilling. He was fearless, almost stupidly so, in the face of authority.

But the day he'd cut open the frog in high school biology he'd known a career that involved blood and body parts was out. He suspected he wouldn't even be able to handle looking at slimy tonsils. Which meant dentistry, an extremely high paying profession, was unfortunately also out. Mark's dad had been a vet. Since Adam had never so much as owned a goldfish, and could not even pretend an interest in the plump poodles that he had seen in Mark's father's outer office, he knew he wasn't going to be doing that either.

Mark's mother had been a psychologist, also a respectable profession, but the money was not as good, and probing the secrets of the human mind when his own was so largely baffling to him left him cold.

Accounting was too dull.

And that seemed to leave law. Nice clean work, for the most part. Though he had seen some slimy things that would put a pair of infected tonsils to shame. Still, he had a good mind for it. He excelled at it. Problem solving. Thinking on his feet. Keeping track of a multitude of different things at once. Butting heads. Maintaining his personal integrity when all about him others were losing theirs. He liked it. It was constantly changing and constantly challenging.

But somehow, even though the workings of his own mind baffled him, he knew becoming a lawyer had been about her.

She had picked Mark because they were from the same world. He had known intuitively that education was the passport to her world.

Education opened doors. Bought nice things. Bought respectability.

He had sworn the next time he was ready to ask a woman to spend her life with him, she would say yes.

The problem was that woman was supposed to be Kathleen. Twice as beautiful as Tory. Ten times as sophisticated.

Tory had already had her kick at this particular can. She'd lost her chance. Picked Mark.

But now Mark was dead.

And Mark had sent him back here.

He closed the briefcase and took the letter back out of his pocket. It was getting soft from so much handling.

He closed his eyes. He really didn't have to read it again.

Mark's last request of him. Make Tory laugh again.

Mark. Handsome. Athletic. Quiet. Stable. A good choice if you had to make one. A sensible choice.

That was what they had both been, Tory and Mark. Sensible. He bet they didn't drink cola at half-past eleven at night.

He took a defiant swig, and suddenly felt so tired he thought he would collapse.

He set the letter on the table, stripped off his clothes and crawled between the soft sheets.

He slept almost instantly.

Chapter Two

Adam awoke in the morning feeling disoriented. Then it came back to him. Calgary. Tory. Mark. A mission.

He groaned, sat up, stretched. He saw the can of cola that he had taken precisely one swig from, and wondered how it was possible to feel like he had a hangover. The letter was beside the cola tin. He picked it up.

Don't read it again, he ordered himself, and then read it again.

Dear Adam:

I asked my lawyer to wait a year before sending this on to you. Tory will need time. We married before we completed university, and she needs to know she can make it on her own.

But she needs to laugh, too.

I know how much you loved her.

And I know she loved you more than me. When she picked me, even though she loved you best, I began to believe in miracles.

You know, I've never stopped.

She was my angel. And now, if things work the way I think they do, I'm going to be hers.

This is my last request, Adam, and only you can do it. Go home. Go to her. Make her laugh. Teach her to have fun again. Rollerblade, and ride bikes with two seats, fly kites, sit out on lawn chairs at the lake and watch for the Big Dipper and Orion to come out.

She was always a little afraid of how you grabbed life with both hands. But she knows a little more about the nature of life, now. She won't be afraid to take what it offers her.

You were my best friend, besides her. I know why you stayed away. She was mad at you, and probably still is, but I wasn't. I'm watching out for you. I promise.

The letter was signed, simply, *love, Mark.*

Every single time he read that letter, Adam felt the same lump of emotion rise in his throat. The last paragraph in particular reminded him with such aching poignancy who Mark had been. Solid. Loyal. Loving. The fact that Mark's handwriting was wobbly with pain, like the writing of a little old man, always seemed to increase that lump in his throat to damn near grapefruit size.

"This was not a good way to start the day," Adam told himself, getting up and putting the letter down.

But the words stayed.

I know why you stayed away. Adam wished Mark would have said why. Because he didn't know himself. A thousand times he had almost come home. A thousand times something had stopped him. And he did not know what that something was.

Pride. Hurt. Anger. Betrayal.

He shook his head. Mark seemed to think it was something else. But then Mark could be wrong. Look at that nonsense about Tory loving him, Adam, better.

When he'd first received the letter he'd known he absolutely could not go to Tory. He had several important trials coming up. Kathleen's sister was getting married, and he was to be master of ceremonies. He had a 1964 Harley panhead in pieces in a friend's garage.

He couldn't just go traipsing across the country to go Rollerblading, for God's sake!

And then he found he couldn't not go.

Mark's last request.

It kept him awake nights. He read over that blasted letter so often that the paper was wearing thin. You would think the lump in his throat would be getting smaller, but it never did.

Tory not laughing? How could that be? Tory *was* laughter.

Finally, he surrendered. The letter was not going to let him go. If he followed Mark's instructions precisely, fulfilling his last wish would only involve four things. He could probably be done with it in four days. A week, tops.

And maybe the mystery in that letter would unravel.

I know why you stayed away.

"Great," Adam muttered, "that makes one of us."

He went and showered and dressed. What did one wear Rollerblading? He put on jeans and a white denim shirt. Everybody in Calgary wore jeans, even lawyers.

He went out the hotel door at quarter to nine. A girl with tired looking eyes, in a worn dress, stood on the corner with a basket of flowers. On impulse he bought them all, and was rewarded with a shy and lovely smile.

Really, it had nothing to do with romancing Tory, he defended himself as he hailed a cab. If she had one weakness, it was flowers, and he needed to get his foot in the door.

At first he thought she had outsmarted him and escaped, just like the little piggies who left for the fair an hour before their appointment with the big, bad wolf.

He banged on her front door, and when she didn't come, he sauntered over to her living room window and peered in.

Somehow he had known before he looked in exactly how it would look—lace and antiques, bookcases, sunny colorful prints, scatter rugs, hardwood, wainscoting, wallpaper, framed petit point, flowers, fresh and dried, hanging and in hand-thrown pots.

Homey and charming. The kind of room in which one sat in front of the fireplace with a pipe—unlit, now that he was reformed—and an old dog at foot, the day's newspaper in hand. It was the kind of room in which one could feel utterly content.

His own upscale condominium was furnished in a look he referred to as modern motorcycle. Black leather and chrome. Somehow homey was not the ambience he had achieved. Or yearned for either.

Until now.

He could hear the faint sound of music and followed it like a dog following a scent, off her front porch and down a narrow swatch of grass in between her house and the one next door. He came to a high fence. No gate. But the music louder.

Vivaldi. Once he wouldn't have known. Or cared.

He glanced around to see if any of the neighbors were watching suspiciously. The street was quiet. The wall of the other house was windowless on this side.

He spit on his hands, tossed his bouquet of flowers over first, and acknowledged a funny little singing inside of him. And then he caught the top of the fence and hefted himself over it, landing with a thud that was drowned out by the music and a delicate looking shrub that he thought might have been a magnolia, though he had never heard of one growing successfully in Calgary.

He shoved a few broken branches back into place, picked up his flowers and looked around her walled yard with interest.

His offering of flowers seemed redundant.

Her backyard was like an English country garden— flowers and shrubs were everywhere, narrow stone paths going between them. He could hear the gurgle of a fountain. He glanced to his right and saw her deck.

It was a work of art, really, multilayered wooden platforms sporting potted trees and barrels of flowers and water, benches and planters.

On the top platform, connected to her house by a lovely set of French garden doors, she sat at a patio table beneath a colorful umbrella, surrounded by wicker baskets full of dried flowers and baby's breath. She was bent over something, her pink tongue stuck between her teeth in concentration, the sun on her hair turning it to flame.

He looked for a place to dump the flowers he had brought. The wilted bouquet was a ridiculous offering given the wild profusion of blossoms in her yard.

She glanced up, saw him, and froze. Then she glanced at her watch, confirming his suspicion that she would have been long gone had he waited for the appointed hour. But, by the look on her face, she had meant to be gone by now, and had gotten caught up in something, become lost in the task at hand.

He went up the stairs toward her, holding out his bouquet, a drooping peace offering.

She didn't reach out to take it, folding her hands instead over her chest, and regarding him with wide brown eyes.

He saw she was working on an arrangement of dried flowers and what looked to be a dried corn stalk twisted into a bow shape. A glue gun was at her elbow. Given the simplicity of the items she was working with, the arrangement was nothing short of breathtaking.

"That's very good," he said inadequately.

She shrugged. "It's what I do. My business."

He sensed even this short explanation was offered to him reluctantly.

"How did you get in here?" she asked.

"I jumped the fence."

For the slightest moment just a hint of laughter leapt in her eyes, but she doused it swiftly.

"Then you can go back out the same way."

He ignored her. "Mark built the deck, didn't he?"

He watched her eyes soften as she glanced around. "Yes."

She still loved him.

Uninvited he sat down, placing the humble nosegay on the table. "He did a nice job of it."

"You know how he loved to build things."

"Yeah. I know." The tree house that had been in progress since they all turned thirteen came to mind. Mark had always been the idea man. The result was a tree house that had been the envy of every boy and girl within a hundred miles. Windows with shutters, a rope ladder that wound up and down, a sturdy deck out the front door.

"Is the tree house still—?"

"Still at my mom and dad's. Being enjoyed by the grandchildren, now. The tree house. This deck. They're all he ever built. He never became an architect. He got sick before he completed his degree."

"I'm sorry." And he was. But the word *grandchildren* was begging for his attention. He looked around for toys, for signs. Surely he would have heard. "The kids enjoying the tree house aren't yours, are they?"

She shook her head, looked away quickly. "My sister. Margie's."

He remembered her sister, Margie, only vaguely. She had been much older than them. Or so it had seemed at the time. Four or five years now wouldn't be quite the same chasm.

"Mark got sick very shortly after we got married."

"Aw, Tory. I didn't know."

"Would it have made any difference?"

He didn't know, so he didn't say anything. She didn't seem to expect him to. Unless he was mistaken, she was still in her pajamas, a kind of fuzzy two-piece short suit with pudgy angels frolicking in the pattern of fabric.

Not intended to be the least bit sexy, he found it unbelievably so.

"Is that coffee I smell?" he asked wistfully.

She glared at him.

"I'll trade you this little posy." He wagged his eyebrows at the flowers, hoping she would laugh.

"You're offering those in trade? They look pretty near to death," she said scornfully.

"The coffee's an unknown. I tried cookies you baked on three or four occasions before I wised up and fed them to old Brewster."

"No wonder that dog was so monstrously fat. I suppose it wasn't just you, was it?"

This was encouraging. She was asking him questions. "Mark, too," he admitted, "and your dad."

"My dad?" She was trying to look outraged, but he thought he could see a bit of smile trying to press out past the prissy set of her lips.

She took the flowers, got up and marched into the house. The shorts were really very short. Her legs were gorgeous. It looked like she could still ride a bicycle fifteen or twenty miles without breaking into a sweat, or shinny up a tree in five seconds flat.

She glanced back and caught him looking. He half expected her to slam the door behind her, turn the key in the lock and then stick out her tongue at him, but she didn't.

She came back out a few minutes later, a carafe of coffee in one hand and an extra mug in the other, a long white terry-cloth robe hiding her delectable little knees from him.

She poured him a coffee as the birds rioted in her yard.

"What a beautiful space you've created for yourself, Tory."

She looked at him uneasily. "I grow most of these flowers for my business."

"What is your business?" He took advantage of the tenuous peace between them.

"I make dried flower arrangements, like this one, and sell them to upscale gift shops like the ones on Kensington and in Mount Royal Square. I have some contracts in Banff, too." There was a hint of pride in her voice.

She'll need to know she can make it on her own.

"You're doing well, aren't you?"

"Extremely. Better than I ever expected. I call my business Victoria's Garden."

He wanted to pull her in his arms and swing her around

at the pride he saw shining in her eyes. But that brought thoughts of what her body, wrapped in the fluffy robe, would feel like after all these years.

Now, for the first time, his mind going down a very dangerous path—thinking wayward thoughts of her—

"Adam?" she asked.

"Coffee's great," he said gruffly, taking a sip. It really was great. Exotic. Like coffee and chocolate and mint all mixed together. "Have your cookies improved?"

"I seem to have better luck with flowers. Adam, what are you doing here?"

"I told you. Taking you Rollerblading."

"But I don't want to go Rollerblading!"

Neither do I, he thought. It was not on his list of the one hundred and one things that he most wanted to do in his life.

"Why not?" he asked, sneaking a look at her over the rim of his coffee cup. She looked beautiful. Flustered, her curls scattered around her face, the freckles standing out on her nose. Her freckles always stood out on her nose when she was upset.

Somehow the purpose of this exercise had not been to upset her.

"I'm too old," she said.

He almost spit out his coffee. "Too old to have fun?"

"Oh, Adam," she said. "I stopped believing life was fun a long time ago."

And then, for the first time, he felt committed to his mission. Knew why he was here, knew why Mark had sent him, and knew that he couldn't fail.

"It must have been very hard for you. Watching him die."

"It wasn't hard at all," she said stubbornly. Her chin tilted up, and her eyes glittering dangerously. "It was

incredible. I didn't regret one minute of it. It was a privilege to make that journey with that strong, courageous
man.''

Her speech finished, her composure crumbled. Silver
tears trickled down her cheeks. She swiped at them impatiently. More replaced them. She covered her eyes, trying to regain control. Her shoulders started to shake. She
hiccuped.

And then she was sobbing. Uncontrollably.

And a voice deep within him, in his soul, told him
what to do. He went and scooped her from her chair, and
then sat back down in it, with her cradled against his
chest. And while she wept, her hot tears trickling down
his shirt, he stroked her hair and murmured words to her
that came from some part so deep within him he had not
been aware it existed.

He told her how proud he was of her for being so
strong. He told her it was okay to cry. He told her he
was going to help her laugh again. All the time aware of
how slight she was in his embrace, how good she
smelled, how soft her shoulders were under his hands.
And all the time aware that she still loved Mark.

That her love with Mark had been one of those loves
that would transcend all obstacles, even death.

And that was good. He was relieved. His future was
safe after all. Kathleen was real and good and eminently
suited to him in every way, and he was going to go back
to Toronto and lose no time in asking her to marry him.

They would buy a house somewhere in suburbia, and
someday they might have children—two point two, just
like the national average.

"How?" Her voice was small, muffled against his
shirt.

For a startled moment he wondered if she was asking

how one had two point two children, which he had not exactly figured out.

"How what?"

"How are you going to make me laugh again?" she asked somberly.

"I'm going to take you Rollerblading," he said.

She flung back her head and looked at him. Her eyes were all puffy from crying. She seemed to realize suddenly she was in his lap, and she scrambled out of his embrace and onto her feet.

"You're not giving up, are you? Just like the old days!"

"Bulldog Reed," he agreed. Her robe had pulled apart slightly below the belt, and he tried for a glimpse of her upper thigh.

"Adam, you have to go away." She looked down, blushed, and pulled her robe ferociously into place, yanking hard on the belt.

"Not until I take you Rollerblading."

"And then you'll go?"

As a lawyer he had mastered a few nuances of lying without actually lying. For instance, you could incline your head a certain way and people took that as assent, when in the letter of the law no verbal agreement had been committed.

He tilted his head, a gesture one might mistake as preceding a nod.

She straightened her robe again unnecessarily, and pointed that cute little nose at the sky and spun away from him.

He waited for the slamming door, the turn of the key, and actually felt relief when it didn't come.

He had finished all the coffee in the carafe before she finally returned, her face scrubbed free of tear stains, dressed in some terribly unattractive sweat outfit in the most unbecoming shade of gray he had ever seen.

Not intending to be the least bit sexy, she was unbelievably so.

"All right," she snapped. "You want to go so bad, let's go." Covering up her moment of vulnerability with cool dignity. With impatience. In her eyes a vow: never to be vulnerable to him again.

He sighed.

Tory watched him get up from his chair. God, he was glorious. He always had been. Incredibly handsome, but more. Sure of himself—and that certainty showing up in the way he moved, pure masculine strength and grace in his every move.

He was dressed casually today, in jeans faded to dusty blue from long and loving wear, and a white denim shirt. It made him look more like, well, *him,* than the expensively dressed man who had appeared on her doorstep yesterday.

His hair was falling carelessly over one eye. Beautiful hair, black and thick and silky. Hair that begged to be touched, begged her fingers to reach up and flick it back for him. She had done that all the time. Before. When his face and their friendship had been so familiar to her. When he'd been a part of her life, like the river was a part of her life. Something she had assumed would be constant and unchanging.

Every woman they saw today would look at him.

In the old days, he'd rarely noticed. Or if he did, he would grin back at them and then turn and give Tory, or Mark, a puzzled look. Like, *What's with them?* or *Is that someone we know?*

And she was dressed in one of Mark's old sweat suits. It looked absolutely appalling on her, and she knew it.

She had started out quite differently. She had marched into the house and past his pathetic flowers, which for some reason she had put in her very best vase.

In her bedroom she had thrown open her closet and scrutinized every outfit she had. And tried on three of them, finally settling on a nice pair of pleated white shorts and a jade-green silk blouse that did the most splendid things to her hair and her eyes. Which, of course, was too ridiculous considering where they were going.

Next had come black jeans and a flannel shirt. Better. Faintly feminine, but hardly alluring. It showed off her coloring and her trim figure rather nicely.

A dusting of make-up and then the fist slamming into her stomach.

What was she doing? Trying to make herself look attractive for Adam! As if her heart wasn't vulnerable enough to those dark flashing eyes.

"The idea," she told the mirror, "is to get rid of him."

Who did he think he was, coming here, casually trying to renew an old friendship, commandeering her life, when he'd abandoned her, *them*, when they needed him most?

He was a dangerous man. He was dangerous to her heart. A heart that was already damaged almost beyond repair.

She had never said it out loud. Mark would have been disappointed in her if she had. He might have felt guilty. Like he had done it to her.

But she said it out loud, now.

"I am never going to love anyone again." And, she added to herself, least of all Adam Reed, who had shown beyond a shadow of a doubt he could not be trusted with such delicate organs as hearts and souls.

And so she scrubbed her face until it shone, and left the freckles and the hollows under her eyes. She combed her hair, but didn't mousse it so that each curl stood out, separate and shining. And in the very back of the closet she had found an old sweat suit that belonged to Mark, and that she had hated on him and that looked even worse on her than it ever had on him.

She went back out onto her back deck, defiant, amazed when in his lazy gaze she saw frank appreciation.

"Unless you want to jump back over the fence," she told him haughtily, "you'll have to come through the house."

She hoped he'd offer to jump the fence. She did not want Adam to see her house. It was too close to her. Reflected her very soul.

And somehow her soul felt like it needed to be protected from him.

He stopped inside her back door, waiting while she slid it shut and locked it.

They were in her kitchen and she turned and tried to see the room through his eyes. Small and cluttered with dried flower paraphernalia. The top of her old round oak table barely visible under a mound of baby's breath and pink ribbons.

He was smiling. "This room says a lot about you."

Just what she feared! "And what is that?"

"The stove looks like it never gets used, but the microwave does."

She slid a look to her stove. Sparkling clean as the day it arrived. The microwave had a little splotch of something red on it. Spaghetti sauce from her last TV dinner.

"And you don't eat at the table, so I bet you eat on

the back deck when it's nice out, which is not that often in Calgary. The rest of the time you eat in the living room. Watching TV. No. Not Tory. Music. Listening to music. And watching the bird feeder you've got in the front yard. And keeping an eye out on the neighbor's renovations and decorations."

She glared at him. A portrait of a lonely and pathetic soul. And accurate.

He'd always been like this, looking and seeing what other people never saw. Incredibly observant and astute, able to take a few telling details and weave out a whole story.

"Did you have to remember that?" she asked grouchily.

"What?"

"That I liked looking at other people's houses."

"Little peeping Tory. You used to love to go for walks at twilight, right as people were turning on their lights but before they closed their curtains."

"A weakness," she admitted haughtily.

He laughed.

She wished that he wouldn't do that. It chased the years from his face and made him back into *her* Adam. The boy next door. That wild boy that she had loved so madly.

In those simple days, it had been okay to love them both. Mark quietly, and Adam wildly. It had always seemed as if it could go on like that forever.

But, of course, she knew better now.

There was no forever.

She marched him through her living room with her head held high, not inviting his comment. But she saw this room through his eyes, too. Suddenly it seemed cramped and prissy, and like a room an eighty-year-old grandmother would enjoy in the evenings with her knitting and her cats.

"No TV," he said with a pleased grin, and then, "I like your house, Tory. I like it a lot."

She held open the front door for him. The doorway was narrow. He brushed her as he went by. She could feel his heat and his strength. He smelled good. She hoped her hand wasn't trembling as she put the key in the dead bolt to lock the door behind them while he held the screen door open.

"Thank you," she said tightly. "Your car or mine?"

"I came by cab. I thought we'd just walk. It's a beautiful day."

It was a beautiful day. To walk with him along the path by the river would be like strolling toward the past. The river had once seemed like it belonged to them, as familiar as their own backyards.

"Are we going to the island?" she asked.

"That's where they rent them. The Rollerblades."

Returning to the old playgrounds of their youth. She did not know if she could stand it.

They crossed Memorial Drive and moved down the path. The sun came through the leaves of the giant trees that bordered the path and dappled the earth around them green and gold. The river looked steely gray and cold.

She noticed with relief that they had nothing to say to each other.

And then with less relief that he seemed perfectly comfortable with the silence.

She did not have to chatter, to think of clever things to say to keep him occupied, to fill the silence between them. Had never had to. With him, and with Mark, she could always just be herself.

Against her will she felt something relax within her.

"Out of the way, Gramps!"

A boy, perhaps sixteen or seventeen, streaked by them on a bicycle. As they leapt out of his way, Adam encircled her with his arms, protectively.

She looked at Adam. And felt warmth in the circle of his arms, strangely like homecoming. She could feel his breath rising and falling, and the beat of his heart. This close she could see the beginnings of dark stubble on his strong chin and on his cheeks. An outraged expression was on his face.

"Are you all right?" he asked, and eased her away from him to look.

"Oh, fine," she said, dusting an imaginary speck off her sweatpant leg, hating herself for how badly she wanted to go back into the circle of his arms.

She glanced at him. Apparently he hadn't even noticed their close encounter, was not stirred as physically by it as she had been. Of course, it had probably not been a year since he had come in close contact with a member of the opposite sex!

He was glaring after the cyclist. "Gramps," he sputtered indignantly. "Did that delinquent call me Gramps?"

She nodded, wide-eyed, trying to repress the giggle inside of her. It would not be repressed.

"What's so funny?" he demanded.

"The look on your face. That boy—" she was giggling now, and because she was trying not to, it seemed to her the sound coming out of her was most undignified. Like snorting.

"What about that boy?"

"He looked just like you used to look, Adam. Devil-may-care" she was laughing now. Laughing as she had not laughed in years. And then she saw the smile on his face, and remembered how his smile had always had the power to change everything. To turn a bad day into a good one, to make a hurt heart feel better.

"Hell-bent for leather," Adam said ruefully, watching her, smiling at her laughter, not seeming to find her snorting undignified at all. "I never yelled at people to get out of my way, did I?"

"Oh, you were much worse than that."

"I was not."

"Yes, you were."

Suddenly he was standing very close to her again, and her elbow was in his hand and his eyes were darkly intense on hers.

"You liked it, didn't you, Tory?" he growled.

And her laughter was gone, replaced by another feeling she remembered all too well around Adam. A kind of walking-on-the-edge feeling, caught somewhere between fear and exhilaration.

"Liked what?" she stammered.

"The rebel in me. The bad boy."

"It scared the hell out of me," she whispered.

She didn't add: *And it still does.*

Chapter Three

"Adam, why are we doing this?" Tory asked him, closing the latches on the apparatuses now attached to her feet. "I never even liked ice-skating. Neither did you!"

"I know. The only boy in Calgary who never played hockey. Probably in all of Canada. An albatross I have carried around my neck for two decades."

"Answer the question then. Why?" She wiggled her feet. Even though they moved on command, they seemed strangely detached from her body.

"I'm tired of carrying the albatross?"

She shot him a look. He had never given a damn what the rest of the world was doing, and he didn't care now. It was written in the supreme confidence with which he carried himself, written in the light that lit those devilishly dark eyes. This expedition was not about whether he had played hockey as a boy.

He rose to his feet, and when his feet scooted out from under him, he grabbed the back of the bench where they had sat to put their skates on, and tried to look casual and in control.

For once he didn't succeed, and it really was quite funny.

"Don't stand up," he advised her. "We'll just sit on this bench and look like we're having a rest."

Damn him. She could feel that little smile twitching again.

"He'll know," she whispered wagging her eyebrows toward the kid who had rented them the skates—the same boy who had nearly mowed them over on his bicycle.

Adam had given him hell for clearing them off the path, and the boy had grinned at him with a certain impish charm and said, "Sure, Gramps, I'll watch that next time."

"I'm not your Gramps," Adam said in a low, lethal tone that had set the hair on the back of Tory's neck on end.

"Yes, sir," the boy had said, not the least perturbed. "By the way, my generation calls them in-line skates, not Rollerblades."

"I think I defended his brother on a murder rap," Adam said to Tory, looking over at the little booth where the boy was now happily engrossed in a comic book. "I'm sorry I tried so hard."

She couldn't help herself. She laughed. "Well, unless you want to be Gramps forever, you had better let go of the bench."

"Ladies first," he insisted smoothly.

Tentatively she tried standing on her feet. "It's like standing on a plate balanced on top of ball bearings," she said when her feet seemed to be going every which way from underneath of her. Bent over from the waist, she grabbed the seat of the bench.

"At least I'm maintaining my dignity, Gran," he taunted her.

She blew a curl out of her way and looked up at him. She let go of the seat, straightened and lunged toward him. She caught him around the waist and held tight.

He stared at her, something darkening in eyes that were already darker than pitch.

Her own heart was quickening within the walls of her chest. It would be a very good idea to let go of him.

But if she did that she'd probably land flat on her fanny in front of him. There was no denying how good it felt to hold him, his muscles strong and sinewy beneath the denim of his shirt, his body throwing off soft heat, like early summer sunshine.

"The little creep is watching us," he said under his breath.

"Then let go of the bench."

He did. His arms wrapped tightly around her.

She was not sure if it was an improvement. Her heart seemed happy. Her head was muttering something about pure insanity.

"Turn right," he ordered tersely.

They inched their way around, and then took a few wobbly steps forward.

"The little creep is laughing."

"Adam, I'm afraid we're hilarious."

A man jogged by, grinned and shook his head.

"Okay," Adam said, "that's it for Rollerblading. In-line skating. That looked like a great restaurant we came by. Let's—"

"Forget it. This was your idea. We've got to take at least one turn around the park."

"Is this park any smaller than it used to be?"

"No."

"Why are you torturing me?"

"Because I tried to talk you out of this and you wouldn't listen. You promised me fun. Laughter."

"Well, they're all laughing." He scowled darkly at a herd of cyclists who went by.

"Adam, you can't lean on me so hard. You're pushing me over."

"I'll take off my skates," he said, brightening, a lawyer who had just found his way out of an impossible dilemma.

"No!"

He ignored her. "And you'll leave yours on. I'll guide you."

"No!"

"You can close your eyes. Pretend you're blind. I'll be your Seeing Eye dog. A laugh a minute. I guarantee it."

"No. Absolutely not, no."

"I hate it when you say that 'Absolutely not, no.'"

"You haven't heard me say it for a long time."

"It doesn't seem that long."

"It doesn't? When did I ever use that expression on you? I never said no to you."

"Yes you did. The night that I asked you to marry me."

She actually felt the blood drain from her face. Of course. The only time she had ever said no to Adam.

"Sorry," he muttered. "I really hate this. Much more than I expected to hate it."

"Are you referring to Rollerblading or something else?" she asked suspiciously.

He sighed, but the melancholy of it was lost when his foot shot off to the right and left him leaning on her drunkenly, threatening to pull them both down. He scrambled to regain his balance.

Adam's dignity had always been innate in him.

He was like a duck out of water with these foolish inventions on his feet, and she could not imagine what had led him to this moment.

He swore under his breath, a word that was pure Adam.

She started to laugh.

He glared at her.

She started to laugh harder.

"Stop it. You're making my skates wobble."

It was the first time she had ever seen Adam so out of his element and so out of control. It was delightful.

She pushed off tentatively.

"Not so bloody fast!"

She pushed with her other foot. "I think I'm getting it."

"Tory, you are going way too fast!"

"Do you remember what you used to do when I said that to you when you took me on motorcycle rides?" she asked fiendishly, pushing hard with her right skate, propelling them both forward. Something was bubbling away inside her. If she was not careful, she might see it for what it was. Happiness.

"I used to say, 'Of course. You're right, Tory. I am going much too fast.' And then I'd slow down."

"Tut-tut, such terrible lies." She pushed with her left foot.

"Not lies! A faulty memory."

"You used to go faster," she reminded him, shoving off again. She was slightly in front of him now, breaking away from him. He clung to her elbow, bent slightly forward at the waist, his knees bent, his feet looking like they were locked together.

"I was young then," he said. "Immature. I wouldn't behave that way now."

"I would." She pushed again. He was so uncooperative that he was knocking her off balance. She was starting to laugh.

"We're coming to a hill," he warned her grimly.

"That's not a hill. A mere bump. You used to jump your bicycle off a dirt heap ten times that high."

"But I was in control!"

"It seems to me you wound up in a cast."

"I broke my bones when I was young, and they mended swiftly."

They swooshed down the little roll in the land. She laughed at the wind in her face, his grip on her elbow. She looked back at him, and laughed harder at the look of grim foreboding on his face.

"I'm laughing," she called to him breathlessly. "You were right! It's fun!"

"Tory, slow down. This is not fun. You are not really laughing. You are having a panic attack that you are mistaking for laughter."

"Try pushing off with your skates, Adam, like this—"

And then they were falling, down and down, all twisted together, landing somehow on the soft green grass beside the path.

And she couldn't stop laughing even though an awful pain was shooting through her knee.

He was so heavy on top of her, his face so close to hers, his eyes dark and black, the whole universe in them—the stars, and the sun, and all the laughter she would ever need.

For a moment she thought he was going to kiss her. She froze underneath him. Wanting it more that she had ever wanted anything. And less. If he kissed her, she knew her world would never be the same again.

In actual fact, had her world ever been the same after that very first kiss from him? "I think I twisted my knee," she stammered, buying time.

"Really?"

"I'm afraid so. Ooh, it hurts."

He rolled off of her and somehow flipped himself around so that he was down at her feet, his Rollerblades wagging in her face.

"Which one?" he called.

She dared to look. He was on his knees and elbows, his rear pointed at the sky.

On anybody else, hopelessly undignified.

On him, sexy, his tight buns embraced by the fabric of those soft jeans.

"Right," she squeaked. "My right knee."

A svelte young woman ran by in silky shorts, had a good look, jogged backward for a few steps.

Gramps was not what she was thinking, Tory deduced blackly.

Adam, just like in the old days, didn't even notice. "I'm just going to roll up your pant leg so I can look."

Tory lay back and looked at the bright blue sky and the huge fluffy clouds above her. She felt him rolling up the leg of her sweatpants, not too difficult since they were four sizes too big. She was wearing a belt to keep them up.

And then his strong hand was on her knee. When had a plain old garden-variety knee turned into such an erotic zone?

"Don't touch!" she ordered through clenched teeth.

His touch became even more tempered with tenderness, causing a terrible twist in her heart and some other places, too, much worse than the one in her knee.

"It's swelling a bit. Does it hurt?"

"Agony," she said of the butterfly tremors in her tummy.

Two women, mid-thirties, very stylish, huge slavering dogs on leashes, sashayed by, laughing loudly and sending not very subtle looks of interest his way.

He glanced up.

One of them smiled.

He turned and frowned at Tory. "Did I know her?"

"I don't know," Tory said grouchily. "Did you?"

He lost interest in the topic. "This doesn't look very serious, but I think our Rollerblading session is over." He tried not to sound too delighted.

"In-line skating," she reminded him.

"Let's see you put some weight on it." Forgetting he had his own skates on, he tried to get up. His left foot shot forward and his right one back. It looked very painful before he crashed.

He said a word, pure Adam, that made the raven-haired beauty going by on *her* in-line skates laugh prettily. She had on shorts that showed off the results of many, many buns-of-solid-iron workouts.

He didn't appear to notice her buns or her laugh. He sat back, undid the fastenings and yanked the skates off his feet. A look of such unguarded and abject relief crossed his face that Tory laughed again.

"That's my girl," he said, "laughing into the teeth of danger. Scoffing at pain."

She felt pain, all right. And it had something to do with the fact she was not his girl. She felt like a traitor for thinking that. Even though Mark was gone. Even though Mark would not have minded. Mark might even have been delighted at Adam's return to her life.

Mark had never known how hard it had been the one time she had said no to Adam.

The truth was she was an ordinary girl. A plain, ordinary girl. And there was nothing ordinary about Adam and never had been. How could he ever have been happy with her?

He had asked her on a whim, one of those impulses he was famous for. The whole thing had been an impulse from the moment he had knocked on her bedroom window at four in the morning to let her know his motorcycle, an ancient foreign model he had rescued from the auto wrecker, was running. Did she want to join him on a test run to Banff? He promised her breakfast when they got there.

The journey had been pure Adam. Exhilarating. Full of the promise of adventure and excitement. And then out of nowhere, he had asked her.

And her heart had cried yes.

But her head had told her she just wasn't an adventure-and-excitement kind of girl. She had been the kind of girl who wanted stability. Life the same every day. Flower gardens and picket fences and tricycles to trip over on the walk.

And so she had chosen Mark. A safe life, and a predictable one.

He had been diagnosed with cancer two weeks after they married.

She had never felt like fate laughed at her. Never. But she had felt humbled. She had come to understand there were things people controlled and things people didn't. That nothing was really safe and predictable at all. Even with the most careful planning.

"Are you okay?" Adam asked, breaking into her reverie, looking at her closely, far too closely, as if he could see into her troubled soul.

She nodded, forced herself to smile brightly. "You know me. Scoffing at pain."

"Arm around my neck, one, two, three, up."

She was up, her arm draped around his neck, feeling surprisingly solid.

"Back to my original plan," he said. "Seeing Eye dog. Hold on tight."

She held on tight. It was the strangest sensation. Like being thrown a life preserver. When she had been totally unaware she was drowning.

"You're in your socks," she pointed out to him.

"Three dollars at the five-and-dime."

"You don't shop at the five-and-dime."

"How do you know?"

"You never even shopped there when you were poor."

Something flitted across his face, and she was sorry she had said that. He'd always been sensitive about the fact he had less money than her and Mark. She thought he would have outgrown it now that he was so obviously successful.

The look was already gone. "I don't care if the socks cost fifty bucks. I'm not putting those things back on my feet."

"Did you see the size of those dogs that went by a few minutes ago?"

"I'll watch. And if I step in anything, I'll—"

"Sue."

They said it together and burst out laughing.

"Are you okay being tugged along like this, or should we take your skates off, too?"

"Nah. I want my money's worth—out of the skate rental and my socks."

He cheerfully pulled her back to the booth. Adam gave the kid such a cold, hard look that he retreated behind his comic book with only one small smug snort.

Adam insisted on kneeling at her feet and pulling her skates off and helping her put her shoes back on.

A couple of elderly women went by and gave her a look of such naked envy that she blushed.

"That restaurant is not very far," he said. "Come on. I'll buy you a hot dog and get some ice to put on your knee."

Say no, she ordered herself. It was over now. He'd promised. Rollerblading and good-bye.

"That restaurant doesn't sell hot dogs. It's not lunchtime, anyway."

"It is where I come from. Come on. We'll have a quick bite to eat, and then I'll piggyback you home."

"You will not!"

"Wouldn't be the first time."

"I weighed about thirty pounds less last time!"

"But so did I."

"It was after that game of scrub when we were in the ninth grade."

"Maybe I weighed fifty pounds less," he said thoughtfully. "God, that was a long time ago. I can't even remember what I looked like."

But she could. Adam, his hat on backwards lean and muscular for a boy that age, stronger than all the rest of them put together. Adam, who could be counted on for at least one home run every game, who could run like the wind and wing a ball in all the way from the Moore's back fence. Adam with that light of pure devilment dancing in his eyes.

She looked. It was still there. Buried deeper, but still there. What was he up to?

"Maybe a hot chocolate," she said reluctantly, and took his proffered hand. It folded around hers, strong and warm, and then he was putting her arm over his shoulder, and she limped painfully along beside him for half a dozen steps or so before he scooped her up in his arms.

"Put me down, Adam. I'm too heavy."

"You weigh about as much as a soaked kitten. Kind of look like one, too."

"We look silly."

"So what? Who knows us?"

He'd always been like that. Other kids worried about what they looked like. Other kids gave in to peer pressure, wanted to be part of the crowd, had to have a certain style of sneakers and jackets. It had only seemed to baffle Adam.

She gave up and nestled into him. Lord, he was strong. "How on earth does a lawyer stay so strong?"

"How did you know I was a lawyer?"

"I heard. Somewhere."

"I'm not really that strong. I'm putting on a brave front."

"Then put me down, you ridiculous man."

"No."

He said the word with that stubborn tone to his voice and set to his chin that meant nothing but trouble.

She sighed.

"What do you call a hundred lawyers strapped to the tracks with the train coming?" he asked her. He wasn't really struggling at all, not even breathing hard. Just striding along with one hundred and ten pounds in his arms.

A plump woman went by pushing a baby carriage. She winked at Tory.

"What?"

"A start."

"That's awful, Adam. Not in the least funny. Aren't you proud of what you've done with your life?"

He gazed down at her for a moment, his brow knit. "Proud? I never thought of it like that. I mean, Mother Teresa led a life to be proud of. Me? I just make money. Lots of it."

"You've become cynical."

"I was always cynical."

"That's true."

"I've just found a way to get paid for it."

"Adam, you're happy, aren't you?"

He looked down at her. Happy. He thought so, really. He was successful. So busy that there were days he had to decide which meal he could most afford to skip. He was in a pleasant relationship. He was rebuilding a 1964 Harley-Davidson.

Happy?

The happiest he'd felt in a long, long time was right now, with her sweet weight pressed into him, and her huge eyes on his face.

Their shared silliness on those damned skates had made him happy.

"Well?" she demanded.

"Yeah. Sure. I'm happy."

She was looking at him with a look he could only call cynical. But they were at the restaurant and he settled her in a chair and ignored her big brown eyes by looking at the menu.

"Berenstain Bear furniture," she said looking around.

The furniture looked like it had all been made out of sticks. "Berenstain bears?" he asked.

"I can tell you don't have much exposure to kids. You

used to love kids. Remember the summer you and me and Mark coached the Hillhurst Hyenas?"

The truth was he remembered it all. Every single time they had laughed together, he remembered.

"Yeah, I remember," he said gruffly, trying to hide behind a menu he was having trouble making sense out of. She ordered hot chocolate. He ordered salmon, and had to surrender the menu.

"Do you remember Hercules?" she asked him.

"The girl who could pop a foul into the river?"

"Miss Calgary two years ago."

"No way!"

He had not wanted to do this. Had planned to skillfully detour any walks down memory lane.

"We won every game, didn't we?" he asked, and he could hear the warmth of the memory in his own voice, remember the kids gathered around them, and her eyes laughing—"

"The male twist on history," she said, shaking her head. Her hot chocolate arrived.

So did his salmon. It looked raw. He wished they'd had hot dogs after all. "We didn't win every game?" he asked, surprised.

"Two. We won two games."

It was a good excuse to spit out the salmon. "No!"

"Afraid so."

"But why would I remember winning all the time?"

She smiled with such softness he knew what she would say before she said it.

"Mark."

Mark. Of course. Such a good sport he genuinely never cared if the kids won or lost, and somehow he managed to make them not care either. It was always fun, and that's what he remembered. The kids gathered around

Tory and Mark and him with joy in their eyes. He'd remembered that, perhaps not surprisingly, as triumph.

"He always took the whole damn works of them for ice cream after," Adam remembered. "Win or lose."

"You used to help him pay for it. And I think that was the summer you stocked shelves at Safeway."

"I helped pay reluctantly. A future lawyer, even then."

"I don't remember you being reluctant."

"A guy tries not to let his inherent greed and self-centeredness show." *Around the girl that he loves.*

But for Mark there had never been any reluctance. He'd loved treating those kids. He would have gladly missed fueling up his car for a few days to do it. The better man.

"He was really a special guy, Tory."

He had to get this over with. Quick. He was feeling lonely and bereft and as if he had missed the most important things in life. He had to get out of here.

Away from her, and her eyes, and her lips touching that mug and sipping the foam off the chocolate.

Instead, he heard himself asking about old classmates and about her mom and dad and Mark's parents, and listening to her replies like a man thirsty, a man who had crossed the desert without water.

"So," he said, "are you free to go bike riding? Tomorrow, maybe?"

He could probably whack them both off in one day, the bike ride and the kite thing. That left only the lake. He could be clear of here by the weekend, with any luck.

She was looking at him as if he had lost his mind.

She pointed at her knee.

He suddenly felt sick, and he didn't think it was the slimy salmon. Tory was not going to be bike riding anytime in the near future.

Or flying a kite, either.

How long? A week? Two?

A week or two back here in the company of all these ghosts? With her so much alive?

He felt like he was being pushed toward some unknown place within himself. A place he had no intention of going. None.

He called for the bill.

She got up, and he saw her face seize up with pain as she put weight down on her knee.

The thing about this island in the middle of the Bow River in the middle of Calgary was that there were no roads on it. That was its charm. No motorized traffic. It was reached by footbridges.

He supposed they could get an emergency vehicle on it somehow, but Tory would kill him if such a fuss was made over her.

He was going to have to piggyback her home after all. And every step was going to just bring him closer to what he used to feel.

"Lawyers don't have feelings," he muttered to himself.

"Pardon?" she said.

He looked at her, and for a man with no feelings, his heart nearly seized right up.

He knew he was in trouble. The biggest trouble of his entire life.

He'd never minded trouble before. But the kind of trouble in those dark-brown eyes was the kind he'd never really been prepared for. It was the kind of trouble a man could not really prepare for.

Not even if he had an entire lifetime to try.

Chapter Four

Adam paced his hotel room. There was actually a trail in the carpet where his footsteps had flattened the nap. He had the ugly feeling that if someone offered him a cigarette right now he'd take it. After four and a half years without one.

He made split-second decisions every single day. He was good at it. Some might even say great at it.

So why was this decision so difficult? Go. Or stay.

He'd piggybacked her most of the way home yesterday. She'd insisted on hobbling along beside him for a few steps every now and then, but mostly he carried her, her coltish legs wrapped around him, her arms around his neck, her whole body crunched up against his back.

Her hair smelled like lemons and her breath like hot chocolate. Who would have ever guessed that this would be a combination his poor beleaguered brain would register as erotic?

They had laughed hysterically, like two little kids playing hooky from school and on their way to the candy store. With a buck each in their pockets.

He shook his head, remembering. He'd whinnied at people going by, just because it made her laugh and pound on his back and demand that he stop it at once. Was that any way for a lawyer to behave? Whinnying on a public pathway?

Okay, so she couldn't go bike riding or kite flying.

He'd made her laugh. That's what he'd come to do and it was done.

Go or stay?

There was absolutely no point staying. None.

Unless he counted the look in her eyes when he'd made the damn fool mistake of touching her mouth when he'd finally set her down in front of her place. What he had really wanted to do was kiss her. The lemons and hot chocolate and twenty minutes of carrying her laughing had all added up inside him, making him stare at her lips once he'd set her down, thinking of only one thing.

Until he'd thought of one other thing. What if he kissed her and it was like kissing Mark's girl?

And yet her lips had looked soft and tender and touchable, and so he had given in, in part. He had touched the silky fullness of her bottom lip with his fingertip instead of his mouth, and even though it made no sense at all, the sensation had stunned him with its intensity.

He had kissed many women, long and hard and thoroughly, and the same things had not been stirred in him that the feel of her lip against his finger stirred.

He shook his head.

Not a reason to stay, if he thought about it. One more reason to go.

Except that he had not fulfilled Mark's last wish. Not to the letter. And somehow back in Toronto, the fact that he had made her laugh was not going to be good enough. The stupid bike ride and kite thing would haunt him. And what was the point of going all the way back if it was going to end up haunting him? He would just end up coming back here to finish it properly anyway.

But what was the point of staying if he couldn't fulfill the remaining requests in Mark's letter? There was no way she was going to be riding a bike or flying a kite anytime soon.

Looking at her lips could damn near drive him insane.

He'd thought of asking her out for dinner last night. Over and over he'd thought of it. The lips that taunted him were exactly what stopped him. He ended up ordering room service and eating lukewarm food over some paperwork. He'd called Kathleen and got her answering machine.

He said hi, things were going well.

Only after he'd hung up, did he notice that he hadn't told her he would be home tomorrow. And that he hadn't told her he missed her. Or loved her.

He wandered over to the window and shoved his hands deep in his pockets. "Aw, Mark," he said. "I don't know what to do."

If he stayed, he had to deal with her lips. If he left, he had to deal with his guilt.

Early morning rush-hour traffic jammed the street below him. A taxi cut off a Mercedes and a horn blared. And then he saw it. Way down there, at the right-hand side of the road, holding its own with buses and cars and trucks.

A ricksha. A bicycle-drawn ricksha.

Without even stopping for his jacket he raced out his hotel room door and took the steps down three at a time.

He burst out the main door. It had been easier to spot that contraption from way up above.

He began running in the direction it had been going.

Even as he ran, he became aware that what had happened upstairs had been a power struggle between his head and his heart. His head telling him to go. His heart telling him to stay.

As a lawyer, he liked to think his heart was an underdeveloped muscle. Thinking. Logic. Those were the powers that won cases. That ruled the world, really.

But his underdeveloped muscle seemed to have a lot of power right now. Why else would he be risking life and limb chasing a ricksha through rush-hour traffic?

Stay, it told him in no uncertain terms as he caught sight of the ricksha, weaving its way through traffic. He put on a burst of speed, and found out his *real* heart wasn't benefitting that much from all the hours behind the desk either. It pumped wildly.

Stay just until you've completed what Mark asked of you, his head told him sternly.

"Yeah, yeah," he said, taking his life in his hands, leaping in front of a car, and into the empty seat of the ricksha.

The driver, pedaling furiously and effortlessly, turned and looked at him. Shocked recognition hit Adam even before the boy spoke, his voice not the least breathless from all his exertion.

"Oh, hiya Gramps. Where to?"

Tory shifted the ice on her knee. An uncomfortably cold wet rivulet ran down her leg into her sandal. She flipped a towel at it and looked at her yard. Her yard in early morning. It always brought her peace.

Even in Mark's final days, when she had come out

here, her soul quieted. Listened. To some voice inside her that said it would be all right. That everything would be all right. The flowers themselves each gave a little lesson in life and death. Growing, blooming, dying. Bringing beauty and joy, and then fading and falling, in death giving nourishment to the next one that would bloom.

But there was no peace in her garden this morning.

Or maybe the peace was in her garden, as it always had been, but it was having trouble penetrating her own frame of mind.

Her knee was sore. She had a zillion projects to complete by Saturday—none that a sore knee was going to prevent her from doing.

So why was she sitting here feeling so resentful of *him?*

Because he'd made her laugh. Fool. Whinnying like a horse every time they went by someone on that path yesterday. Until tears were rolling down her face, she was laughing so hard.

But then when he'd put her down in front of her house, there had been something in his face that had chased all the laughter away.

He'd reached out and touched the fullness of her bottom lip with his finger; something in that small touch so full of reverence and longing had made her think he would kiss her.

And her whole insides had glowed warm as fire.

But he had not kissed her. Just shoved the offending hand into his pocket, given her a casual salute with the other one, and walked swiftly away, calling a casual "See you later" over his broad shoulder, a shoulder she knew intimately after holding on to it for dear life for the past half hour. But not as intimately as she would like to know it, a little voice inside her own brain taunted her.

Nonsense. He had left the impression that he might phone and ask her out for dinner.

She'd rehearsed saying no a thousand different ways for nothing, because he had not called.

There were lots of reasons for saying no. She was busy. He couldn't just expect her to put her whole life on hold because he'd arrived in town.

Plus, it would be disloyal to Mark to want to spend time with the man who couldn't even find time to come to his friend's funeral.

And, that finger on her lip had opened a whole new dimension to things. A physical side that she remembered all too well.

When she was with Adam, something *sang* in her. And trembled. And wanted. It had been like that since she was about fourteen. Even after she had said yes to Mark, that restless thing had been within her.

Hadn't she been relieved when Adam left town? Relieved even when he didn't come back? Hadn't that feeling of relief been there all the time? Right beneath the recriminations, and the anger that he had abandoned Mark, had she not been just a little bit thankful?

She limped over to a flower basket and yanked a finished petunia head off with completely unnecessary viciousness.

He hadn't called and asked her for dinner. *That* was the kind of guy he was. He was probably on his way back to Toronto by now, without even a call to say goodbye.

Even if he wasn't, she didn't like this. Questioning her own character. Feeling strangely off balance. Feeling this quivering excitement in her belly every time she thought of him...

And she thought of him far too much. Last night in her bed thinking tormented thoughts of his broad shoulders underneath her hands yesterday, her legs curled around him, his scent, wild and clean, filling her nostrils and making her ache, heat rising within her.

She ripped off another wilted petunia head.

Thump.

She whirled and hurt her knee. There he was, lying sprawled out on this side of her fence, his face planted in the dirt.

Don't laugh at him, she warned herself grimly.

He got up. A smudge of dirt was on his cheek.

"Oh, hi," he said casually, as if he had bumped into her at the dry cleaners.

Her heart was doing this traitorous little dance inside her chest. And she was smiling. Even though she didn't want to. At all.

"Oh, hi," she said, and then added even though she didn't want to, at all, "Fancy meeting you here."

He laughed, and came up the stairs toward her, two at a time, all his incredible energy shimmering around him.

"How's the knee? It doesn't look great."

"It doesn't feel so hot, either." She looked at the dark head bent over her knee, and shivered. *Don't offer him coffee.* If she'd been so convinced he was halfway to Toronto, why had she made enough coffee for two this morning?

He straightened, and even though she didn't want to, at all, she reached up and brushed the dirt from his cheek. Her fingers lingered. His eyes lingered. And then he kissed her fingertips and she snatched her hand away. "Do you want coffee?" she stammered.

He'd kissed her fingers! And she offered him coffee! Instead of telling him to get lost. Instead of telling him to go back to where he came from.

She looked reproachfully at her fingers, as if they were entirely to blame for what had just come out her mouth. They were. They burned pleasantly where his lips had touched them. She wiped them energetically on her knee-length denim shorts. It didn't help.

"I'll get the mug." He went in her house and she could hear him rummaging around in there, whistling.

She sank down on the plump cushion of her patio set. What would it be like to have Adam rummaging around in her house every morning, whistling?

Until she had heard that sound it was like she hadn't been aware of a space in her life chock-full of emptiness.

Adam's whistle felt as if it could fill that space, as if there would be no more loneliness. How had she managed to so successfully outrun the knowledge that she was lonely?

Dangerous thoughts. He lived a million miles away. She knew nothing about him, anymore. Nothing. He probably had a girlfriend, or a dozen of them. Maybe he even lived with someone. Isn't that what everybody did now?

Why did she care? He was leaving. She was staying. Two very good reasons not to care if he had a girlfriend. Two very good reasons not to be planning too much around the cheerful notes of his whistle.

"Adam," she called, even though she didn't want to, at all, "Do you have a girlfriend?"

Silence.

"Adam?"

He came out the door and set down his coffee mug, carefully. "I see someone."

She knew, without having to ask, that they didn't live together. Somehow that would not be Adam. He had always had such an innate sense of integrity. And she knew something else, and was surprised by how well she knew him, still.

She knew he did not love her, the one he was "seeing," even if he had told himself he did.

And she felt relieved, and then angry with herself for being relieved.

Adam Reed was simply none of her business. Not his life. Not his girlfriend.

So why did she hear herself asking, "What kind of motorbike do you have now?"

His face suffused with a light that the girlfriend had not given it. "It's a 1964 Harley panhead."

"An old bike?"

"Who would want a new one? All you do is ride them. I'm completely stripping and restoring this one. It used to be a police bike. Look. I've got a picture of it."

He dug through his wallet, leaving a heap of credit cards and business cards on her table. No picture of the girlfriend, she noted, as she took the photo of the motorcycle from him.

The bike was a thing of beauty with its black paint and shining chrome. She noticed it was a single seater.

His someone that he was seeing did not go riding with him. She handed him back the picture and watched him try to squeeze everything back into his wallet.

Really, her coffee was done and so was his. It was time to bid him a polite farewell. Really, it was.

But her garden felt so good again. The sun out, and the flowers blooming in profusion, the birds singing, his quiet voice weaving around her, making her feel the way she used to feel. Safe and happy, and like all was well with the world.

"And what about your dad, Adam? How is he?"

"He remarried shortly after I talked him into moving out east with me."

"Really? That's wonderful." How fondly she remembered the tall, handsome man who had been Adam's father. Adam had gotten his looks from him, and his build. But his father's nature had been quiet, almost shy.

"I remember your dad seeming sad," she said softly.

"He loved my mom. I thought he'd never stop missing her. Sometimes raising a kid on his own just seemed too much for him. Especially a wild one."

"You never talked about your mom. I mean you said she had died, but that was all."

"I guess I never really stopped missing her either."

She glanced at him with surprise. Sadness had not seemed to be a part of Adam Reed, ever. But maybe sadness was where that wildness had stemmed from. It occurred to her, with more surprise, that there were things she did not know about Adam. Depths she had not explored.

And never would, she told herself firmly.

"So your dad's happy? He must be retired by now."

Adam laughed. "He married Hanna Oldsmith."

She shook her head. The name meant nothing to her.

"Old money. One of the richest women in Ontario. Possibly in Canada."

Somehow that picture did not seem at all ludicrous, because Adam's father had always had a quality much like Adam's. Dignity, despite his shyness, a way he carried himself that had belied the grease embedded in his hands. "Did you introduce them?"

"No. He worked on her cars. You know my dad. Not the least impressed with her money. That was a first for her. She chased him relentlessly. I don't know why he ran so hard from his own happiness. Anyway, I got a postcard from them last week. They're driving a reconditioned Packard across North America. "

"I always liked your dad. He was so sweet and self-effacing. I'm glad he's happy."

"Me, too. Look, should we go?"

"Go?" she asked suspiciously. "Go where?"

"For a bike ride."

"Motorbike?" she asked with surprise.

"Bicycle. Or as close as I could come, given the shape you're in."

"Adam, are you going through a second childhood, or what? You seem to want to do all these strange things. In-line skating, bike riding—"

"Kite flying," he suggested smoothly.

"Anyway, you know I can't."

"If you could, would you?"

She smiled. A safe question. If she could, yes, she'd ride bikes with him. And probably fly kites with him. And go to the moon with him.

But she couldn't. "If I could, I would," she said, feeling perfectly safe in her reply. She didn't like the light that leapt glistening to life in his eyes. Had she just walked into a trap?

"Victoria? Are you here?"

"It's Mom," she told him and then called, "Out back."

Her mother came through the back door, and paused when she saw Adam. "Oh," she said, "I'm sorry, I didn't realize—" and then she stopped and stared at him. And then her lip trembled and her eyes actually sparkled with tears.

Her mother had always loved Adam as if he was her very own son.

"Adam," she said softly, her voice breaking. And then she smiled a smile that would have put the sun to shame.

A smile that forgave him all the years he had not come, Tory thought indignantly.

"Lord, what a man you've become."

Trust her mother to *say* it.

"Come here."

He got up obediently. He towered over her mother now, and tolerated her inspection, and then he took her in his arms, picked her right up off her feet and swung her around until she was laughing breathlessly, like a young girl.

"Do you still make the best chocolate chip cookies in all of Calgary?" he asked her putting her away from him and looking at her with pleasure.

"So my grandchildren tell me. Tell me everything. If you're married and have children. What you're doing here, how long you're staying—" she stopped mid-sentence. "Oh, I can't stay. I have an appointment. Never mind. I'll cancel."

"Mom," Tory said imploringly.

Her mother looked at her, and then back at Adam, and then smiled. "Of course I won't cancel! Why you two must have so much catching up to do!"

Tory stared at her mother in horror. She had not been hinting they wanted to be left alone, only that the interrogation should stop!

"Adam, will you be here tomorrow night?"

Tory watched out of the corner of her eye and felt something in her relax when he said he would.

"Come have dinner with us? Please? Oh, Frank will be so thrilled. You wouldn't mind if I asked the Mitchells, too, would you? I know they'd be over the moon to see you.''

The Mitchells—Mark's parents. She saw him hesitate, and then he smiled and said yes, he'd like that very much.

"Oh, Tory, you come too,'' her mother said casually, as an afterthought. "I do have to go. I just stopped to give you that begonia. It's got to go in quick. By the way, what is that thing parked out front?''

"What thing?'' Tory asked.

"That thing belongs to me,'' Adam said.

"What thing?'' Tory asked again.

"Did you hurt your knee, honey?'' her mother asked, noticing the ice pack.

"Yes. What thing?''

"How did you do that? It's hard to hurt your knee making flower arrangements.''

She glared at her mother for letting Adam know, not very subtly, that her daughter didn't have a life. Her mother knew darn well she could fall down the steps as easily as anyone else.

"I went in-line skating,'' she said defiantly.

"In-line what?''

"Skating.''

"Skating,'' her mother said with pleasure. She shot a look to Adam. "Did you have anything to do with this?''

"Well, yes ma'am, I did.''

"Uhm,'' she said, somehow managing to load that noncommittal word with lots of satisfaction. She glanced at her watch, gave a quick and unconvincing cry of dismay and, with a quick wave, left them.

"She didn't give a fig about my knee,'' Tory said, glaring after her. "And what have you got in front of my house. Some kind of disreputable bike?''

"Yeah. But not my normal kind. A pedal bike. Kind

of like a bicycle built for two, only this one is for one person with good legs and one person with a bum leg."

"What are you up to?"

He sighed. "Tory, I don't even know anymore. Just come for a damn bike ride with me, okay?"

"Well, since you put it so nicely," she agreed. And found she wanted to. A lot.

He helped her up. They left the ice in the sink. She saw the ricksha and burst out laughing.

"Adam, have you lost your mind?"

"That would explain it as well as anything else. Madam, your chariot awaits you."

"All right. But no whinnying. Absolutely not. If you whinny, I'll throw myself under the tires. I swear I will."

"No whinnying," he promised solemnly.

He helped her down the walk to the ricksha. It looked as if it was going to be a great deal of work to pedal this thing.

She noticed her neighbor's new drapes, and decided they weren't as bad as she had originally thought they were. Her neighbor seemed to be peering out from them now. She waved jauntily and climbed into the carriage part of the ricksha.

Her plan for the day had been not to get any further enmeshed with him, she reminded herself. To set boundaries. To send him packing.

She settled herself back and watched as he climbed onto the bike. How long had it been since she went into a day with no plan at all? When had she become this person who had to compulsively control every second of every day? She suddenly felt deliciously free.

"Want to hear the horn?" he called.

"Why not?"

It sounded just like a donkey braying. She wondered if it was possible to die from laughing. She hoped so.

Her mother, he thought, as he pulled out onto the road, was a beautiful woman. She looked exactly how Tory was going to look in maturity. Really, it was something a man could look forward to.

He had never thought of Kathleen's mother in terms of what Kathleen would someday be. Why was that?

The ricksha felt like it weighed precisely the same as a baby elephant. He glanced back at Tory. She was smiling. She waved at some open-mouthed children riding on their tricycles on the sidewalk.

"Race you," she called to them.

They took up the challenge, racing along the sidewalk beside him. He beat them by a hair to the end of their block. Actually, the ricksha weighed more like a mama elephant than a baby one.

"Blow the horn for them," she called.

He blew the donkey bray for the children who howled with delight. He glanced back at Tory. She looked delighted, too, her face relaxed, glowing.

He pulled off her block and onto Memorial Drive, looking for a chance to cross to the bike path. A horn blared at him. He blared his back. The driver shook his fist, and Tory waved.

He wasn't sure he could get the ricksha across the grass to the bike path even if he did manage to get across all four lanes of traffic and the boulevard. He decided to block one lane of westbound traffic instead. He got quite thick-skinned about the horns blaring. He was glad the road was relatively flat. A hill would finish him.

Some teenage boys slowed down their sports car and

were flirting with Tory, which backed up traffic behind them.

Didn't she know she was much too old for them? Didn't they know?

But the look on her face right now was without age. She looked like a little leprechaun, her curls wild, her nose freckled, her wonderful eyes dancing with life and laughter. It was exactly the look that had always made Tory a big hit with the guys, not that she'd ever seemed to notice, content with Mark's company, and Adam's.

Elephant nothing. The ricksha felt as if he was pulling a 747 behind him.

"Move on," he yelled at the guys. If they called him Gramps, he wasn't going to be responsible for what happened next.

They laughed and yelled a few more good natured remarks at Tory, which made him see red, and then drove on, a stream of cars moving by with them.

Tory smiled and waved at a yellow bus full of schoolchildren that thundered by.

"Wave, Adam," she called.

"Can't," he panted.

How had he gotten himself into this? It was unbelievable. A man of his stature pulling a ricksha. Not just a ricksha, but the world's heaviest ricksha.

He'd gone about three blocks. Had Mark's letter stipulated how long a bike ride?

He glanced back at her again. Damn, if it wasn't worth it. She looked the way she used to look. After their baseball team won a game. After a banana split. After she aced an exam. After she threw rocks at that dog that attacked her, and hit him square between the eyes, making him run away yipping.

The siren wailed once, nearly in his ear, and he glanced

swiftly to his left to see the squad car pulling along beside him, the red and blue lights flashing.

He glanced at his passenger in the rearview mirror that was stuck to his right handlebar. Now she was bent over double laughing.

Adam stopped. Gratefully. He hoped this was going to take a while. So he could catch his breath.

The policeman got out, young and full of himself. Adam would have made mincemeat of him in court, but suddenly all that mattered was that Tory was happy. It occurred to him that this was Mark's thing, and he would try and do it Mark's way. With calm and courtesy.

And so he said nothing in his own defense as the policeman told him he was obstructing traffic. After all, he was on holidays.

He held out his hand for the ticket, grinning like a schoolboy. The policeman glared at him, and went back to the ricksha, assessing its roadworthiness.

"Ma'am, did you hire this man? Did he solicit your business?"

"He is a solicitor," she deadpanned. "I think you should arrest him immediately."

The policeman seemed to figure out they were in it together. It was Adam's turn to laugh, which earned him a look from the young officer. But rather than being loaded with an authoritarian threat, the look held the beginnings of reluctant amusement.

He remembered Mark's way was often like this—hostile situations defused. Turned around somehow.

Adam's way, way back when, would have been to get himself arrested on some point of pride. And he wasn't sure how much he'd changed. He loved making these guys into mincemeat on the witness chair.

The policeman came forward. "Are you, like, romancing your girl?" he asked in an undertone.

"I'm making her laugh," he surprised himself by confiding. "It's been a long time since she laughed."

The policeman looked back at her. "It looks like you're doing a pretty good job of it. How come she hasn't laughed in a long time?"

Adam hesitated. He really didn't have to tell him anything. Mark's way, he reminded himself. "Her husband died."

"That's rough."

"Yeah. He was a good man. The best." Adam felt his throat tighten and looked away.

When he looked back, something had softened in the policeman's young face and he put away the ticket book. "Why don't you just take it over to the bike trail across the street?"

"I was going over there," Adam said, "but I didn't want her to *die* laughing, and I couldn't get across all the traffic."

The policeman shook his head. "I'll stop the traffic for you."

"Hey, thanks."

"You a lawyer?"

"Yeah. How did you know?"

"Her remark about the solicitor finally sunk in. Remember this next time you're going to make mincemeat out of a poor working sap like me, okay?"

"You got it." It occurred to him that when Tory was around love shimmered in the air. It always had. And it changed things. It had always done that, too. That was what Tory and Mark had had in common. A wonderful decency that changed everything they touched for the better.

What had he done lately to change anything for the better?

He didn't think making the juvenile delinquent who had rented him the ricksha into a millionaire counted.

With Tory waving like a queen, they crossed the four lanes of traffic that the young man stopped for them. The cop pushed the ricksha from behind so that Adam could get it across the grass and up the hill to the wide paved path.

"Try not to push anyone into the river," the policeman advised, shaking his head, and darting back across traffic to his vehicle.

They rode along for an uneventful mile or two. The river made a swishing noise, and the birds sang.

It occurred to him that despite the fact he was pulling a ricksha that weighed nearly as much as his hotel, he felt stupidly happy.

The tire blew out on the front of the bike and nearly sent them over the bank into the river.

He gave up. "Stay here," he ordered her.

"Gladly," she said, and sank back against the bench of the ricksha and watched contentedly as the runners and the river moved by her.

He looked at her. Maybe Mark's idea was working. She seemed to be happier than she had been yesterday. Much happier. The light seemed to have been switched back on in her.

He dashed across the street to some nifty boutiques and bought a plaid blanket and a basket of goodies from a deli. He spread them out on the grass beside the broken chariot.

"Did you get smoked oysters?" she asked, pretending hauteur.

"Of course. And liver pâté. The caviar didn't look fresh, though."

"I can't stand that when the caviar isn't fresh," she said. She went into his arms as easily as if she'd been born to them, and he carried her to the blanket, and set her down. He pulled the cork on the bottle of sparkling water, and offered her the first swig. She took it, wiping her mouth happily, and passing it back. She rummaged through the basket.

"Oh! You really did get smoked oysters!"

"Really." He drained the bottle and pulled out another one. "Jeez, that was hard work."

"You're getting soft."

"I know it."

But she didn't think he looked soft at all.

"You're still crazy."

"I know that, too."

Her lip trembled, and she looked away. *I've missed you.* But she did not say that out loud.

He moved very close to her, his shoulder touching hers companionably. "Don't go and spoil it all by looking sad."

"I just wished Mark could be here with us."

"Maybe he is."

Chapter Five

Adam lay back on the blanket. The sun was warm on his face. He felt full and drowsy. The river ran by. Birds sang. The leaves on the trees seemed to be shiny and new, a vibrant shade of green he felt he had never seen before. June seemed to have a scent of its own—fresh and new and full of promise. It occurred to him he had not taken a holiday, felt this relaxed, in years.

Tory was lying beside him, not quite touching him. It was the inner debate about whether to move that half inch or so closer that kept him from going to sleep. He could inch over ever so casually, and then his shoulder would be touching hers.

It occurred to him he was putting a lot of mental work into a shoulder touch. And it occurred to him he'd rather touch her shoulder than go a lot faster and further with any other woman. Including Kathleen.

She was wrecking him. Tory was wrecking his whole life. And she was doing it without making even the tiniest effort.

He somehow doubted that while she was standing in her shower this morning, she'd been applying that lemon scented shampoo, thinking, "This will drive him wild. He'll go straight back to Toronto and break up with that someone he's seeing."

He supposed he'd have to kiss her to find out what her breath was like. Oyster kisses. Unappealing with anyone else. With her, the very thought, unbelievably appealing.

"You've changed in some ways," she said decisively.

"I dress better?" He edged closer.

She rolled over and regarded him, his quarter-inch gain lost.

"You do?" she teased, sitting up on her elbow. "You always wore jeans and T-shirts."

"Hey, these jeans cost enough that you were supposed to notice the label."

"Okay, okay, I noticed the label."

And then she blushed. Ha. So she'd been sneaking peeks at his backside. Just as he'd been sneaking them at hers. Maybe she did have an ulterior motive when she was shampooing her hair!

"I wasn't talking about *material* things," she told him sternly.

"Then in what ways have I changed?"

"The way you dealt with that policeman. Once you would have smarted him off until he was all red in the face and jumping up and down—"

"And I wouldn't have given up until I got led away in handcuffs," he agreed dryly.

"So, you've matured."

In the last half hour. "Don't we all?" he said sagely.

"Do you remember that time we got pulled over after that school dance? You got so huffy, said it was just because we were young and that they didn't have any legal right to pull us over.''

"The seeds for my future planted that very night," he said. "I still get pulled over when I ride my Harley. And they still don't have any legal right to do it. I hate that. Law-abiding citizens being harassed because they choose to ride motorcycles.''

"The speed limit?" she probed.

"Oh, that," he groused.

"You always had such a well-developed sense of justice, of what was fair. I shouldn't have been so surprised that you became a lawyer.''

"Were you surprised?"

"Yes.''

"What did you expect me to become? A drug dealer?''

"Adam! What an awful thing to say. I've never even known you to have a beer!''

"A gangster?''

"Adam!''

"I guess I just wondered if you expected something disreputable of me.''

"Not at all.''

"Then what?" he pushed, wishing it didn't matter to him what she had expected. But it did.

"I expected you to have a life of high adventure," she said huffily. "You were kind of a wild boy. Completely untamed.''

"Give me a clue. I'm trying to think of respectable jobs for untamed people.''

"Astronaut.''

"I don't like flying!''

"Cowboy.''

"I'm not too great with horses, either.''

Her look silenced him. "Entrepreneur," she said, "Safari leader. Spy. Firefighter."

It seemed to him she had given this some thought. It seemed to him she saw him as a rather romantic figure. He felt momentarily pleased, until he remembered he had let her down.

"I wasn't that wild," he said.

"Adam, you skipped 92 percent of grade twelve."

"That wasn't because I was wild. I was bored." He'd still passed. It had hardly seemed like high adventure at the time. Shooting pool at Grady's. Working on his bike. On the odd occasion he got it running, actually took it somewhere. Perhaps that had seemed wild and risqué to a goody-two-shoes like her.

"You were wild," she said firmly.

"In what way?" he challenged.

"You rode the chute down Glenmore Dam in a tube."

"Very stupid. Not necessarily wild."

"You jumped your bike off the cliff over by where the radio station used to be."

"It wasn't a cliff, exactly. Besides, I broke my flipping arm and had to get stitches."

"You still have the scar."

He touched his chin. "Do I?"

"And you were jumping your bike off that same cliff a week later, with your arm in the cast!"

"I'd forgotten about that." But he remembered now. It hadn't been a cliff. Just a big, built-up ramp of dirt with a pile of sand at the bottom of it on the other side. Sand that appeared softer than it actually was. Still, the hardness of the landing had not prevented him from going at it again, his arm out of the sling but still in the cast.

It must have been a day much like this one, because

he could remember with absolute clarity the feeling of freedom as he approached the edge, that wonderful airborne moment when the bike left the earth and joined the sky. He sighed happily.

"Just as I suspected," she said. "It's a *happy* memory for you."

He couldn't deny it. But he seemed to remember the light in her eyes spurring him on to ever greater heights of daring. "You liked it, too."

"I did not! It scared me to death when you were reckless and foolhardy."

But that was not the whole truth, and he knew she knew it by the gentle blush that rose in her cheeks.

"You were spellbound," he said. He waited for her denial, but it did not come. Instead, she changed direction.

"You smoked."

"I mistakenly thought it was cool. Not wild. Cool."

"First one in the river every year, and last one out. First one arrested—the *only* one arrested."

"That wasn't really my fault. I didn't know Murphy had stolen that car."

"I wasn't allowed to walk on the same side of the street as Murphy."

"There you have it. The good girl and the bad boy. Natalie Wood and James Dean. It happens all the time."

"Are you admitting you were wild?"

It was more like he was trying to get her to see the missed opportunity. "Maybe I appeared a little wild to a girl like you."

She laughed. "Now you sound like a lawyer."

"Which I am. Not a wild guy at all anymore. And you seem disappointed."

"Not disappointed," she said quickly. "Adam, I just

always thought, of all the people I knew, you would grow up and be something different. That you would be free, somehow. Unfettered by convention. Or expectation.''

''I guess I always thought that, too,'' he admitted. He wondered how much convention had played a role in the decisions she had made, the man she had chosen to marry.

''Well then, what happened?'' She said that with the faintest edge of accusation in her voice, as if he had let her down.

Her. The one he'd chased respectability for.

''I matured,'' he said. ''Grew up. Faced the facts.''

''What facts?'' she demanded.

That Mr. Respectable got the girl.

''There's no money in circumnavigating the globe on a Harley.''

''It is not all about money.''

''That's easy for you to say. You've always had it.''

''Well, you appear to have it now. Does it do the same things to your soul that talking about going around the world on your motorbike used to do?''

He glared at her. It sounded like she would have liked him better if he'd stuck to boyhood plan A. Which ticked him off royally, since plan B had had a great deal to do with her. And Mark. And their neat and tidy little worlds with degrees on the walls and picket fences around their yards.

If he'd offered her that, instead of a motorcycle trip around the world, maybe she'd be Mrs. Reed right now.

''Adam?''

He glanced up, shaded his eyes against the sun.

A slender, beautiful blonde stood there smiling at him.

He hoped this freckle-faced little monster beside him noticed how radiant that smile was.

"Shauna?"

"First-year law," she said, pleased that he'd remembered. "How are you? Still in Toronto?"

"Guilty. Just back for a little R and R."

"And this must be your wife."

"No." *She turned down her motorcycle trip around the world.* "This is my friend, Victoria Bradbury."

He felt Tory stiffen beside him, and give him a look, before she rose to her knees and offered her hand to Shauna.

"Victoria *Mitchell,*" she said, sending him another look.

Of course he knew she'd married Mark. His head knew. Had his heart never accepted it? Is that why he had never even once thought of her last name being Mitchell now, instead of Bradbury?

"Sorry," he muttered under his breath.

Shauna chatted for a few minutes, but he didn't really hear her, aware of Tory's annoyance with him, aware the picnic was over.

"How could you?" Tory asked him softly, when Shauna had left.

"I just forgot. I'm sorry."

"It's just as if he never was to you, isn't it?"

"That's unfair."

"I was married to Mark for six years. You can't pretend that never happened. Why do you even want to?"

"I said I was sorry, okay?"

"No, it's not okay," she said furiously. "None of this is okay. This picnic is not okay. That thing," she pointed to the ricksha, "is not okay. Skating yesterday was not okay. You betrayed Mark. How could I forget that? Let alone forgive it?"

She hopped up off the blanket. She was shaking she was so mad.

It reminded him of the time he'd told her that her chairing the school charity fund-raiser was a waste of her time. The world was not going to change because their high school adopted one starving kid.

"But maybe *we'll* change," she'd cried at him, right in the middle of a hallway teeming with people on their way to classes. Mr. MacKenzie, the math teacher he despised, had had a good laugh over that.

She looked that mad right now, her freckles standing out on her face, her eyes shooting sparks. She turned and began to limp away.

"Does this mean kite flying tomorrow is out of the question?" he called after her, hiding his own fury in an uncaring tone.

She threw him a killing look over her shoulder and kept going. Damn her, was she going to limp all the way home?

Who cared? He'd become a lawyer for her, and she'd told him she would have preferred he rode his bike around the world. Yeah, right. She'd said no to that quick enough.

So, he hadn't made the grade with her then, and he still didn't. *Now* he could go back to Toronto. He'd done his best. Made a mess of it, but his best, nonetheless. He wasn't Mark. He didn't have his gift for diplomacy, his ability to fix things broken.

And the truth was, Tory was broken.

And in some way, so was he.

And riding bikes, skating and flying kites was not going to fix what was broken between them.

Trust. It was the trust that was gone.

He had trusted her with his heart, and she had said no.

And she had trusted him to do the decent thing when Mark was ill and he had not. There. Unfixable.

That night the police had pulled them over after the high school dance, and he had mouthed off so badly he'd nearly been arrested, Mark had fixed it. With the right word and a friendly grin, by just being who he was.

But Mark wasn't here anymore.

He closed his eyes and lay back, his arms folded under his head. When she glanced back, she would see a picture of uncaring.

He opened his eyes when something wet plopped on his face.

"I don't have cab fare," she said proudly. "I can't walk."

She was crying on him, but she would have been even madder if he noticed, so he pretended not to. Without sitting up he fished in his wallet and handed her ten bucks.

"Mark forgave me."

The sound of his own voice stunned him. He had not meant to speak to her. He had meant to let her go. Meant to get on the next flight back to Toronto.

He peered up at her.

"Mark forgave you?" she whispered. "How could Mark forgive you? You never even—"

He fished in his pocket again, handed her the well-worn letter.

She unfolded it uncertainly, glanced at him, and read the letter.

When she was done, she threw it down on him.

"This is why you came back?"

He nodded, but her tone already told him sharing the letter with her had been a mistake.

"Because you felt sorry for me?"

"Because he asked me to!"

"Not because you really cared about me at all! Because he asked you to!"

"Tory—" he started to sit up.

"You couldn't do the decent thing all by yourself? And I did not love you better! I didn't!"

An elderly woman going by with a poodle looked over at them, ducked her head uncomfortably and hurried by.

Tory gave him a look that could have stripped paint, and then turned and limped away. A cab came by, and she held up her hand and the damn thing stopped.

He watched her get in it, her nose pointed regally at the sky.

"Buddy," he told Mark, "we are really blowing this thing." *Okay, me. I am really blowing this thing.*

She had always had the temper to go with that hair. Fiery. Quick to ignite. In a few hours, she'd probably feel contrite. That would be the best time to ask her about the kite.

Or maybe tomorrow night at her mother's dinner which the Mitchells were going to attend. He wondered if they were as angry with him as she was. If they, too, felt he had let Mark down.

Let's face it. He and Tory were never going to fly that kite.

He wanted to go back to Toronto. Where he'd made this nice boring life for himself and hardly ever even thought about going around the world on a motorbike anymore.

But he knew he wouldn't.

He'd realized when he'd landed in Calgary that the part of him that wanted to do the right thing was under-developed. That the man he'd become would have looked at this mess and just cut and run. Now, only three bloody days later, he knew he couldn't leave without seeing the Mitchells.

They had been so good to him when he was growing up.

If he had hurt the Mitchells as much as he had hurt her he wanted to tell them he was sorry for that.

It wasn't quite up there with saving starving children, but it was enough out of his comfort zone for him to send a wary glance heavenward.

But he had no sense of Mark being out there somewhere, looking down at him.

Instead, he had an even more disconcerting feeling—that all that was best about Mark survived. His kindness, his compassion, his courage, lived on.

In him, in some deep and secret place within him, lived all that was best about Mark.

"Because Adam would throw this bike right in the river," he said. "And the blanket and what's left of the picnic." Instead, he folded the blanket. He placed it and the remains of the picnic on the seat and began the long push back.

The kid was just closing his rental stand on the island when Adam got there.

"Aw, man, what did you do to it?"

"It's only a flat tire."

The boy looked distressed. It made him look younger.

"Shouldn't you be in school?" Adam asked.

"Sure. My lucky day. The guy who breaks my bike is the truant officer."

"I just wondered. The bike isn't broken. It only has a flat tire."

"School's a bore," the kid told him, getting on his knees to inspect the tire.

"Yeah. Been there. I'll give you a hand with the bike. Maybe we can get it to the nearest service station."

"That's a million miles from here. I've got a kit at home for fixing the tires."

"Okay, so I'll help you get it home."

The boy hesitated enough for Adam to know what home was going to look like before they got anywhere near the place.

And then the kid shrugged. "If you want."

"What's your name?"

"Daniel. Danny."

"Mine is—"

"Gramps," the kids said and smiled with huge delight. Adam shook his head. "Yeah. Gramps, it is."

The house was meaner than Adam could have imagined. The front porch looked as if it was falling off. Hungry looking cats kept coming out from under it. The roof didn't look like it had a hope of keeping water out. One window was boarded up.

"Thanks," the boy said proudly. "I'll take it from here."

Adam hesitated. If he offered to pay for a new tire now, in front of this tumbling-down house, Danny's pride would be wounded, and the fact that the boy possessed pride was written all over him.

"Do you know where I can get a wheelchair?" he asked, instead.

"For a price you can get anything," the boy said without hesitation. "What do you want a wheelchair for?"

"I'm going kite flying with an invalid."

"You want me to provide the kite, too?"

"You have to promise me you won't steal them."

"What do you take me for? I'd have to knock over a cripple to steal a wheelchair. I have scruples, you know."

"I can tell," Adam said. Sincerely.

The boy looked pleased by the sincerity. "I'll have them by tomorrow at noon. You can meet me at the skate rental booth. Fifty bucks."

"Get real." There was no sense in having the kid thinking Adam was going to be a sap just because he'd seen he lived in a run-down house.

Daniel looked pleased by that, too. "Okay. Twenty-five. But don't expect much of a kite for that."

What did it matter? He wasn't really going kite flying anyway. Not unless there was really such a thing as divine intervention.

"I'll meet you at five," he said. "Then you can go to school."

"Lots of money in that," Daniel sneered.

"How much do you make at your booth?"

"A percentage of the rentals."

"That must be a lot on a weekday."

"Okay, it's not great weekdays. That's why I supplement it by driving my ricksha on Electric Avenue. Once the weather gets cold, I'll head back to school, if they haven't kicked me out by then."

"You know the kind of living you could make if you stayed in school?"

The boy tried not to look interested.

Adam leaned forward and whispered a figure in his ear.

"For a day?" Daniel asked, round-eyed.

"For an hour," Adam replied.

Tory got home and gave the cab driver the whole ten dollars, though the fare was only three. Adam really hadn't pedaled very far, which seemed like one more good thing to hold against him.

Imagine Mark writing him that letter. She couldn't believe it. She felt so betrayed and hurt.

By both of them.

Mark said he knew why Adam stayed away. And that he knew she loved Adam better.

Oh, it made her so mad.

In the whole six years they'd been married, they had never had a fight. In all the years she had ever known him, she'd never fought with him.

So different from Adam, whom she recalled scrapping with all the time.

Because he was so maddening.

But Mark. How could he?

She went to retrieve her ice pack. It had melted in the sink, and she had to satisfy herself with frozen peas out of her freezer. Make her laugh, indeed. Get her injured was more like it! Okay, she had laughed a little bit. It wasn't all that great. There was more to life than laughter.

She thought of Adam lying beside her on that blanket and shivered. Wasn't that really when she had started to question why she was there?

When his scent had wrapped around her and made her so aware of him. Aware that if she just moved half an inch, she could touch him. Feel the hard length of his body against her own.

She'd turned over on her elbow and looked at him, and been awed all over again by what an incredible looking man he was.

She was fighting something. Something deep and physical, an almost primitive longing.

And she had done her damnedest to turn it cerebral again. Done her damnedest to make the longing go away by finding fault with him, acting as if his becoming a lawyer was some sort of betrayal of himself.

And then she'd rediscovered how much she liked crossing swords with him. It only deepened that sense of wanting something more from him—that part of him that was fierce and untamed had nothing to do with his motorcycle. And everything to do with the uncivilized glitter in his eyes and the wild promise of his lips.

It was a good thing that woman had come along. And brought her right back down to earth.

They weren't teenagers, anymore, she and Adam, exploring that tantalizing sizzle between them with a certain cautious innocence, both of them scared to death to follow it to where it promised to go.

She had married Mark.

Because she loved him. And from the moment she had said yes to Mark and no to Adam, everything had changed forever and for all time.

Just because Mark had died didn't mean they could start all over at sweet sixteen. She didn't want to be as guilty as Adam. To just pretend Mark had never been alive.

It was awful. She was ashamed of herself for having given in and gone skating with him, climbed in the back of that ricksha.

Even if it had been Mark's stupid idea! Not Adam's.

That just made everything worse. All the confusion, everything intensified.

She limped down the hall to her bedroom and flung open her closet door. She was going to dress to the absolute nines tomorrow when she went to her parents' for dinner.

To the nines.

He was going to see that she was not a woman to be pitied.

He was going to regret that it was pity and not passion that had brought him back here.

It occurred to her, given the events of today, she really didn't have to go to her mother and father's for dinner.

And it occurred to her nothing, but nothing, would keep her away.

The Bradburys lived where they had always lived. And so did the Mitchells. Adam locked the door of the rental car, the wheelchair folded safely away in the trunk. He paused in the gathering darkness and looked at the houses from his childhood.

Of course they were still here. That was the kind of people they were. They stayed.

His old house had been given a face-lift. New windows and new shingles and great landscaping. And yet the feeling was so strong that if he went and looked over the back fence, there would be a motorcycle there.

And a boy, too. The boy he used to be.

The boy who had envied the stability of these families living on either side of him. Had he known, even then, that they were the kind to stay, and he was the kind to go?

A restlessness in him, back then.

Tory called it wild.

But it had been something else. Searching.

And it was only in looking back that he knew he had come as close as he would ever come, here on this street, to finding what he searched for.

A boy who had lost his mother.

So evident now that what he had searched for was love.

And he thought he had found it. Not just in Tory, but in Mark, too, and their families.

Until the moment she had told him no. She wouldn't marry him, she wouldn't travel around the world with him astride a Harley, with her arms tight around his waist and her head buried in the back of his shoulders, the wind tangling in her curls.

What a thing to even ask her, knowing that she was the kind who stayed.

He made himself walk up the narrow walk to the brightly lit house. He had a bottle of a most correct wine under his arm, though he never drank.

He was aware he felt just a tiny bit afraid.

He rang the doorbell, and her mother came to the door.

When he stepped inside the fear went away. It was still Tory's house, even if she didn't live there. It smelled wonderful—of pine cleaner and furniture polish and good things cooking.

Her mother took the wine and her father came and was pumping his hand, and telling him how good it was to see him.

In the living room, he could see the Mitchells sitting on the sofa. He stepped back from her father.

And then they were coming toward him.

Mark's mother looking so much older, and his father with a stoop to his shoulders that had never been there before.

He looked for recrimination in their eyes as they looked at him.

He saw only warm welcome. Happiness. Almost as if he was a favored son they had not seen for a long time.

Handshakes became hugs.

"I'm so sorry about Mark," he said. "I'm so sorry."

"Thank you," his mother said with dignity. "We know you are."

How could they have known that?

He took a deep breath. "I'm sorry I didn't come."

"You're here now."

And somehow that seemed to be loaded with an expectation. That somehow he would fix something.

He knew what, even before the soft knock came at the door.

They all loved Tory. They all thought—

He turned and watched her come in the door. His eyes nearly popped out of his head.

She was wearing a little black dress, that swished around her thighs and had the dinkiest little straps on her shoulders. Dark stockings disguised her swollen knee.

Her hair was tamed.

She had on makeup.

She looked gorgeous and grown-up.

He supposed he looked all grown-up, too, in his expensive suit, and his shirt and silk tie.

Somehow, he had expected she would not come.

And he did not know what it meant that she had come. And that she had come looking like this.

He only knew that everyone else faded from the room, and his throat went dry when he looked at her.

And he knew no matter what happened here tonight, or on the remainder of his trip here, he was never going to marry Kathleen.

Chapter Six

Tory glared at the bottle of wine he had brought. It was easy to focus all her resentment on that bottle of fancy cabernet. It was a very proper choice. Moderately expensive. Tasteful. Boring.

She glanced across the table at him. *He* was so proper now. Looking relaxed and suave in a suit that was a perfect match for the wine. Expensive. Tasteful. Boring.

He glanced away from Agnes Mitchell for a moment, caught her looking, and smiled.

Maybe not so proper. In that smile lurked the boy who had jumped that bike off the edge of a cliff with one arm already in a cast.

And who had never needed to get his boldness from a bottle.

Spellbound, he had told her of the way she had watched him, and it was true. When he had done those wild, reckless things he had done, she had been spellbound.

Of course she'd also been so frightened her breath had

nearly abandoned her body, but another part of her had soared with him. Was entranced by his daring. Maybe had loved that about him best of all. The way he laughed into the teeth of life. Approached it with boldness and daring and fearlessness.

"Tory, dear, you're frowning," her mother, sitting on her right, said to her in an undertone.

She made her lips smile even though it made her face feel as if it was molded out of Plasticine.

And now here he was, with his boring old wine, in his boring old suit, being boring.

Except that he wasn't being the least boring.

They were all as spellbound as she had been.

Now the cliffs he leapt from were legal ones, and yet the daring and boldness were still there, taking on a different form now, being applied to a different world, still making him shine and stand apart from the rest of them.

The suit was navy blue, with a faint gray pinstripe in it. On anybody else it really would have been unremarkable. On him it was sexy, and terribly so.

There was no such thing as a sexy suit, she grumbled to herself. It occurred to her it was what was in the suit that made it seem so—his broad shoulders perfectly fitted under the expensive fabric, the brilliant white of the shirt making his skin look tanned and healthy, and his eyes even darker than they really were. The tie was already slightly loosened around the strong column of his throat.

She squinted at the tie. It looked conservative at first. A closer inspection showed the pattern in it to be motorcycles.

He was relating the story of his first encounter with a judge, and Agnes Mitchell was laughing until the tears rolled down her cheeks. Not even Tory could begrudge

WELCOME TO THE
CASINO:

Try your luck at the Roulette Wheel ...
Play a hand of Twenty-One!

How to play:

1. Play the Roulette and Twenty-One scratch-off games, as instructed on the opposite page, to see that you are eligible for FREE BOOKS and a FREE GIFT!

2. Send back the card and you'll receive TWO brand-new Silhouette Romance® novels. These books have a cover price of $3.50 each in the U.S. and $3.99 each in Canada, but they are yours to keep absolutely free.

3. There's no catch. You're under no obligation to buy anything. We charge nothing — ZERO — for your first shipment. And you don't have to make any minimum number of purchases — not even one!

4. The fact is, thousands of readers enjoy receiving books by mail from the Silhouette Reader Service™ before they're available in stores. They like the convenience of home delivery, and they love our discount prices!

5. We hope that after receiving your free books you'll want to remain a subscriber. But the choice is yours — to continue or cancel, any time at all!

So why not take us up on our invitation, with no risk of any kind. You'll be glad you did!

Play Twenty-One For This Exquisite Free Gift!

THIS SURPRISE
MYSTERY GIFT
WILL BE YOURS
FREE WHEN YOU PLAY
TWENTY-ONE

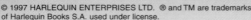

It's fun, and we're giving away *FREE GIFTS* to all players!

PLAY ROULETTE!

Scratch the silver to see that the ball has landed on 7 RED, making you eligible for TWO FREE romance novels!

PLAY TWENTY-ONE!

Scratch the silver to reveal a winning hand! Congratulations, you have Twenty-One. Return this card promptly and you'll receive a fabulous free mystery gift, along with your free books!

YES! Please send me all the free Silhouette Romance® books and the gift for which I qualify! I understand that I am under no obligation to purchase any books, as explained on the back of this card.

Name: _____
(PLEASE PRINT)

Address: _____ Apt.#: _____

City: _____ State: _____ Zip: _____

315 SDL CTHG

215 SDL CTG9
(S-R-08/99)

The Silhouette Reader Service™ — Here's how it works:

Accepting your 2 free books and mystery gift places you under no obligation to buy anything. You may keep the books and gift and return the shipping statement marked "cancel." If you do not cancel, about a month later we'll send you 6 additional novels and bill you just $2.90 each in the U.S., or $3.25 each in Canada, plus 25¢ delivery per book and applicable taxes if any.* That's the complete price and — compared to the cover price of $3.50 in the U.S. and $3.99 in Canada — it's quite a bargain! You may cancel at any time, but if you choose to continue, every month we'll send you 6 more books, which you may either purchase at the discount price or return to us and cancel your subscription.

*Terms and prices subject to change without notice. Sales tax applicable in N.Y. Canadian residents will be charged applicable provincial taxes and GST.

If offer card is missing write to: Silhouette Reader Service, 3010 Walden Ave., P.O. Box 1867, Buffalo, NY 14240-9952

BUSINESS REPLY MAIL

FIRST-CLASS MAIL   PERMIT NO 717   BUFFALO NY

POSTAGE WILL BE PAID BY ADDRESSEE

SILHOUETTE READER SERVICE
3010 WALDEN AVE
PO BOX 1867
BUFFALO NY 14240-9952

NO POSTAGE
NECESSARY
IF MAILED
IN THE
UNITED STATES

her that. It had been so long since they had laughed, any of them, like this.

So long, actually since they had been together as a group, Mitchells and Bradburys. Not since that awful day when they had all stood together in the rain, and each had taken a turn with the spade, putting Mark, their beloved, in the cold, hard ground.

And now they were together again, and laughing, and they could thank him. Adam. The one who had not come.

Did it count that he was lessening the burden of pain *now?* She thought somehow it did, though the admission came grudgingly to her.

Her father cleared his throat, and lifted his glass of wine. "I'd like to propose a toast."

Tory felt his eyes on her, and then his gaze moved to Adam, his intent evident. She felt dread. She knew they were matching them up together, Mark's parents and her own, seeing Adam as heaven-sent. In the bright light of hope that shone in her father's eyes, she could see them being marched down the aisle together. Her father was going to propose a long and happy life to them, and she was not going to be able to live with the embarrassment—

But he didn't say anything about her. Or about Adam.

He said, "I'd like to propose a toast to the man missing from our table tonight, but never from our hearts."

They all picked up their glasses—she and Adam only water—and raised them.

"To Mark," her father said.

And suddenly it was as though Mark were there with them.

She had the oddest sensation of actually *feeling* him—his solidness, his warmth, his great capacity to love.

And when she glanced across the table at Adam, her

animosity seemed to have dimmed. She saw what two pairs of parents were seeing—that he was one of the special ones in the world and it was good that he had come back here.

Their glasses clinked and their eyes held, and it seemed to be his voice only that she heard say, "To Mark."

Then Adam laughed. "Tory, do you remember the time we had that toast in the tree house? I think we were christening it. With Kool-Aid. And you hit Mark's glass so hard it broke?"

"It wasn't *I* who hit it so hard, it was *you*."

"Was it? I think I've improved slightly since my novice attempts at toasting," he said. "Anyway, Mark got cut, and then we saw it as an opportunity to become blood brothers—"

"And then you both came in to me, bleeding like stuck pigs," her mother remembered fondly.

The floodgates opened. And Tory watched and listened as they talked about Mark, remembered him, did what they had needed to do for so long.

Adam, she thought, his blood brother, bringing him back to them. Was it possible he could not have done this if he had been there all along? That perhaps this was his role to play, and that maybe after all, she did not know what was best for everyone and everything, even though she certainly liked to think she did?

"Adam, when are you going back to Toronto?" Sam Mitchell asked him, after talk of Mark had finally subsided, leaving only the warm glow in its wake.

Adam slid her a look. "I'll be on the first plane out in the morning."

She felt her fork freeze halfway up to her mouth. From the look on his face, she suspected he would have gone tonight if he had been able to get a flight.

"Oh, sorry to hear that," Sam said. "I was hoping we might have a chance to fish that spot we both used to favor."

She had forgotten that. That for all his bent toward bold adventure, Adam had always been far more willing than either Mark or herself to spend a quiet day fly-fishing with their fathers.

"I thought," she could not believe the voice was her own, traitorous thing, "we were going kite flying."

If her own behavior had not come as such a complete shock to her, she might have felt some small satisfaction in the fact she had, for once, shocked him.

His mouth fell open and he stared at her.

She glared back at him. Mark's last request—and Adam was going to even try and renege on that?

She was aware of her parents and the Mitchells looking at her oddly.

"Kite flying, dear?" her mother said hesitantly. "Surely Adam doesn't want to—" She looked at him as if trying to make Tory see the fine cut of the clothes, the sophistication.

But Tory wanted to see something else.

The measure of the man.

He tilted his water glass at her, and something glittered dangerously in his eyes. "Kite flying it is," he said smoothly, without missing a beat. "There's nothing in Toronto so pressing as to keep me from a day with a kite."

His eyes said what his mouth did not. *And you.*

She felt a shiver pass from her head to the bottom of her toes.

"Really, what has gotten into the pair of you?" her mother asked. "Those funny newfangled roller skates, that contraption in front of your house yesterday, kite flying. Are you trying to recapture your childhoods?"

Suddenly Tory felt weak. It was not, she realized, about recapturing childhoods, but about recapturing something else.

Something Mark had always known about.

She wished she could take back the reckless words that would keep Adam from boarding his flight tomorrow.

She felt like she was foolishly venturing out onto very dangerous ground. The proverbial thin ice gave a loud crack and groan under the weight of her anxiety.

"Oh, gosh," she said, impatiently aware of how weak her voice sounded, "my knee. I guess I won't be able to go after all."

"You won't have to run," he assured her.

"Even I know you have to run to fly a kite," she said crossly.

"I've looked after it." His tone warned her he was not going to argue with her in the company of her parents and Mark's.

How could he have looked after it, when he had thought he was leaving?

She wasn't quite sure how this had happened. How everything had turned around so quickly and against her will. She had come here tonight to make him pant with longing for her, and then to walk—limp—away with her head high, and alone.

Instead, she had *asked* him to go out with her. Kite flying. Something she had never ever done and had never felt the least inclination to do.

Especially not with a knee out of commission.

It was almost enough to make one believe in divine intervention. If it was not so damn obvious that he was about as opposite to an angel as you could get.

After dinner, he offered to help with dishes, but of course her mother wouldn't hear of it.

"Would you mind then," he said wistfully, "if I went and had a look at the tree house?"

"Of course not," her mother said. "Why don't you go with him, Tory?"

"Yeah, why don't you, Tory?" he asked, grinning at her, as if he knew all about that thin ice she was skating across.

"I'm hardly dressed for—" she closed her mouth. It occurred to her, glumly, that they would always see her as the kind of girl who shinnied up trees, even if she was wearing an incredibly sexy five-hundred-dollar dress.

And it occurred to her she wanted to revisit this part of their history with him.

He held open the door, and they went out into the backyard. The night was warm. The scent of hyacinth and honeysuckle was heavy in the air. The moonlight washed the world in silver.

It was the kind of night where magic happened.

If there was any such thing.

They made their way across the yard to the base of a huge maple. A rope ladder swayed gently in the evening breeze, inviting them up into the canopy of leaves.

"I'm not going up first," she told him.

"You always went first!" he said, mistaking her hesitation for fear.

Impatiently she gestured at the dress, and the light that had kindled in his eyes when she had first walked through the door blazed to life again.

He took a step toward her, and she found herself leaning toward him.

He's going to kiss me, she thought, and was suddenly

aware of how every fiber of her being yearned for his kiss, his touch—wanted it, needed it.

Her strap had fallen off her shoulder, and he gently tugged it back into place, his hand lingering on the soft flesh of her shoulder.

And then he stepped back and laughed softly—the sound was rich in the darkness of the night. "Tory! Would I look up your skirt?"

"Yes!"

He laughed again. "If opportunity knocked. Okay, I'll go first." And he scooted up ahead of her, going up that rope ladder like a sailor up the rigging of an old sail ship. He turned at the landing and offered his hand back to her.

She took it, and again felt some physical response that bypassed entirely the confusion of her mind. *Her hand was meant to be in his.*

Magic. They stood on that small deck, surrounded by whispering leaves, the house lights and the moonlight filtered now.

She was almost unbearably aware of the power in his hand, the electrical feeling that was pulsing through her.

"Do you remember, Tory?"

She remembered.

He looked down at her, and again she was struck with the sensation that a kiss was only seconds away. Instead, he let go of her hand and bent to get in the door of the tree house.

She followed him. It was remarkably unchanged. An overturned wooden box for a table. A crooked shelf holding some crockery and some books. Three beanbag chairs still showing the dents left by the last people who had sat there.

He was looking at the books. "Our copy of *The Out-siders* is still here."

On rainy afternoons they had sat in here and read aloud to each other. They took turns picking books. She had tortured Mark and Adam with *Little Women* and romance novels.

"Trust me," she'd told them. "You'll find out what women really want."

"Sheikhs?" Adam had muttered, disparagingly.

But they had listened, both of them, and enjoyed more than they ever let on.

Mark had liked humor—Robert Newton Peck, Mark Twain, Stephen Leacock, O. Henry.

And Adam liked everything. *Zen and the Art of Motorcycle Maintenance.* Poetry. History. How-to. And the little book he was holding that had become their all-time favorite, which they had read and reread about a dozen times.

"You can take it, if you want," she told him now as he took it off the shelf and despite the darkness, flipped through pages, squinting, reading silently, smiling a little bit.

"No." He put it back. "I'll leave it for your nieces and nephews to enjoy one day."

"Enjoy? I used to think that was the saddest book ever written."

"You used to cry absolute buckets at the part about Southern gentlemen having nothing on Johnny. Have you read a sadder one now?"

She did not say the words. *I have lived a sadder thing now.* Two best friends in the whole world. Mark dead and Adam gone. In the soft gray light of the afternoons they'd spent cocooned here in their private shelter, who could have guessed their future held such things?

She didn't have to say anything, he read it in her eyes. He came close to her, tilted her chin, looked in her eyes, and then closed his arms around her.

She knew she should not allow this embrace, this intimacy, but her bones and blood and fiber and muscle had wanted nothing else for too long, and they mutinied against her mind.

Her mind said pull away, and she snuggled closer.

Feeling safe. Feeling as if the world might be safe again someday, if she let it. But depending on Adam for that feeling would be a very dangerous thing. He didn't live here. He wasn't staying here.

She could probably become addicted to feeling his arms around her, and then he would leave.

Even Mark, Mr. Dependable, had left.

His lips touched her forehead.

Pull away.

But she didn't. Instead she lifted her face and looked at him. It was true then. The feeling she had since they had come into the backyard was true.

He was going to kiss her.

And he did. He rained small kisses on her cheeks and her neck and the top of her head and the tip of her nose.

Hungry kisses. Kisses that had missed her and could never get enough of her. Kisses that spoke of loneliness and empty nights and thousands of days away.

And then his lips found her lips.

And she answered him. With kisses that spoke of a heavy heart being given wing again, and of a fallen spirit being lifted up on the breath of hope.

Kisses that seemed to catch fire some place deep within her before they even found their way to his lips.

Desperately, she pulled away from him, before kisses turned into something that was harder to take back.

"Don't ask me to apologize," he said darkly. "I won't."

"I just don't think that it's a very good idea."

"Actually, it's not bad as ideas go—two lonely people, finding themselves in a romantic setting, sharing a kiss. Big deal. We're thirty years old."

She didn't know what bothered her the most—his accurate assessment that she was lonely, or his assessment that the kiss, which she had a feeling would haunt her into old age, was no big deal to him.

Or maybe it was his own admission of loneliness.

He moved close to her. "I'm sorry," he said. "You're right. It was a mistake."

They went back outside, but instead of going down the ladder, he sank down, his back propped against the wall, his legs bent.

Though she knew she should go, she sank down beside him.

When she shivered, he mistook it for cold and took off his suit jacket and wrapped it around her naked shoulders.

"Where are you, Adam?" she asked softly, when the silence drifted around them, and she could hear leaves, new and vibrantly green, rustling against one another.

His eyes went to her lips, and then he looked away.

"Time traveling. Remembering the three of us and the things we did here. Pirates. Cowboys. Indians. Bad guys and good guys. Cops and robbers. Tarzan."

"Don't forget the Three Musketeers," she told him softly.

"How could I forget the Three Musketeers?" he agreed solemnly. "Those were good days. Full of openness and innocence."

"Love," she said simply.

"Yeah. Those were the days that prepared us for the

world, Tory. Filled us up. Fueled us. Made us strong enough for all that life would give us.''

"I thought jumping your bike off cliffs was what prepared you for life.''

"I guess I did, too, back then. I thought I needed something else. Speed. Adventure. Age has shown me differently. I had—'' his voice cracked, "I had everything I ever needed back then. You. Mark.''

She kissed him again, gently, on his cheek. This time with a blessing. Knowing he needed to go now where all those memories were beckoning him to go.

To do what the rest of them had already done.

She left him in the tree house of his youth, to grieve the passing of his best friend. When she glanced back at him once, from the top of the ladder, she could see the silver tears carving ghostly passages down his rugged cheeks.

Adam set down the phone. Kathleen's answering machine *again*. He felt an urgent need to talk to her.

Not that he'd be such a cad as to break up with her over the phone, but he had to let her know it was coming. Didn't he?

Four days and no answer at her place. Not even late at night.

Not that that meant she wasn't there, only that she wasn't answering the phone. She was probably immersed in preparation for a case.

"Okay,'' he said to himself, "so maybe you are a cad.'' Because part of him was glad she wasn't answering her phone. Uncertain yet of what to say.

Maybe not ready to burn his bridges.

But even as he entertained that notion, he knew it not to be true.

His bridges had been threatened from the moment he had seen Tory again, and recognized within himself the impossibility of ever feeling about anyone the way he had felt about her.

His bridges had gone up tonight. Irrevocably. Irretrievably.

The minute he had seen her in that dress, the bridges had begun to smoulder. And when he had given in to the temptation to taste her lips, the bridges had smoked and then burst into flame.

He'd told her it was no big deal strictly as a defensive tactic. Now, he felt a creeping sense of despondency.

Wanting Tory was like being given a life sentence. Because she didn't want him or care about him in the same way. She had responded, but she had pulled away. She was hungry. Physically hungry. But not for him. For Mark, still?

And he had to take her kite flying tomorrow, and to the lake after that. And not press her for more kisses, not even think about her lips, the sweet wild honey taste of them, if he planned to keep his sanity.

The way he was feeling now reminded him of those desperate days after she had told him she was going to marry Mark.

His world, as he knew it, over. Ended.

For a while, he had tried to stay, to pretend everything would be as it always had been.

When that hadn't worked, he'd attacked his career plans with a furious energy. He moved into the top position in his university class, had seen Mark and Tory only rarely.

And when that hadn't worked, he'd tried running. But two thousand miles hadn't been far enough, and he realized now he could go to the ends of the earth and it would never be far enough.

Time had eventually dulled the pain in his heart, but it had never gone away. When he'd heard Mark was sick, he had applied himself to work with a new and feverish energy.

And when he'd heard Mark had died he had finally allowed that place in him, that belonged to those tree house afternoons, to die, too.

Or so he had thought.

Until he came back here and realized it hadn't ever died, really. Just slumbered. Waited. His feelings—the whole jumble of them—waited for him.

And she, the main cause of all these tormented feelings, had not let him go. Instead she'd had the nerve to ask him to go kite flying! With something haughty and superior in her voice as if she thought his giving up was just another example of his poor character.

But she'd kissed him like a woman with no reservations about character.

And then she'd proven that after all these years she still knew his heart better than anyone else ever had. Because she had left him precisely when he needed to be left. Left him to grieve for Mark Mitchell and afternoons of shared laughter and quiet companionship in a tiny house among the leaves.

The woman was going to drive him crazy.

If he had any sense of damage control at all, he'd call the airport right now and see what flights were leaving tonight or in the early hours of the morning.

But he didn't.

He lay down on his bed, folded his arms behind his head, kicked off his shoes. And remembered that moment when her Dad, Frank, had proposed a toast to Mark. He recalled the silence that had come over the room, and the sudden feeling he had of that silence filling up with peace. He had felt it again, in the tree house, after he had wept until the well within him was dry. He could feel it now. A kind of warm, peaceful feeling. He didn't have to worry about tomorrow, just this moment.

And in this moment, he felt good. As good as he had felt in a long, long time.

He closed his eyes and, fully dressed, he slept.

Tory heard him coming. He was whistling, and he was no better at it than he had been as a teenager, the sound sharp and barely detectable as "Jingle Bells," the only tune, to her knowledge, that he had ever whistled.

She was on the back deck and when she didn't hear the doorbell, she turned her attention on the side fence.

The flowers flew over first.

Followed by the scrabble of his legs. She watched as he paused, balanced at the top of her fence, then bounced over, landing on his feet. He picked up his flowers, and took up his tune, looking quite pleased with himself.

"You're getting pretty good at that," she said reluctantly.

He grinned, noticing her, that Adam grin. "Practice makes perfect."

"You didn't need to bring me those," she said as he came toward her holding out the flowers. "The other ones aren't dead yet."

"Uh, well—"

She studied him carefully. His face looked more relaxed today. He looked refreshed and young and full of mischief. She guessed he had wrestled some demons last night, when she had left him alone in the tree house, and that he had won.

"Where do you keep finding these bouquets so early in the morning?"

"Oh, around."

"A street vendor," she guessed. "You feel sorry for someone selling flowers!"

He actually blushed. "She looks all worn out and she's just a kid."

"Oh, Adam," and she buried her face in the bouquet.

"No big deal," he said.

Just like that kiss last night, she thought, eyeing him. Maybe things were bigger deals than he wanted people to believe.

She had thought she would go to bed last night and be tormented by thoughts of him and that kiss and where things were going, but that had not been the case at all.

She had resolved that they would finish together the things Mark had requested. Be, in some small way, the Three Musketeers once more.

And then she would say good-bye to Adam forever.

Put him in her box of memories along with Mark and get on with her life of making dried out old flowers into something. Puttering around her house. Spying on her neighbor's renovations and decorations. Perhaps she'd get a cat to keep her company.

"So, how does one fly a kite without running?" she asked, pouring him a cup of coffee.

He took a deep and appreciative sip. "You'll see."

And in a while she did. He had rented a car she thought was called a Rattlesnake.

"Viper," he corrected her.

"Why didn't you rent a motorcycle?" she asked, a trifle wistfully.

"Because they don't have trunks."

"And what did you need a trunk for?"

"The wheelchair."

"The what?"

"The wheelchair."

"Are you joking?"

"No."

He pulled the car in at one of the parking lots for the North Hill's Centennial Park. He hopped out, opened the trunk and pulled out a wheelchair.

Laughter, fresh and pure as a brook, bubbled deep within her.

"That chair says Scarlet Leaves Rest Home on it," she pointed out, still laughing.

He looked and muttered something under his breath. "Get in."

She hesitated. Oh, why not just give herself over to this lovely madness? It was only for a day or two more.

And it was for Mark.

Or maybe for herself. For that part of herself that had forgotten how to laugh, just as Mark had said.

She settled herself in the seat, and he handed her a strange object that looked like a brown paper bag mounted on planter sticks.

"What is this?" she asked. It had the cutest picture painted awkwardly on the front—a dragon with bulging eyes and fire coming out his mouth.

"It's a kite."

She looked at it more carefully. "Is this going to fly?"

"I doubt it."

"Did you make it?"

"No."

That was something of a relief. Where would he have gotten the obviously used nylons that adorned the straggly string? "I hope it didn't come from the nursing home."

"Me, too. Or the local kindergarten class."

"So, what do we do now?"

"Hang on for dear life," he advised, and began to race top speed, down a paved path that pitched steeply down a green hillside.

Chapter Seven

"**A**dam! You are going way too fast! Adaaaam!"

"Throw the kite up in the air. Let out the string. More."

Tory managed to wrench her eyes away from their scary descent down the hill and look behind her. Adam's black hair was swept back from his face and his eyes shone with laughter. The kite was actually lifting, swaying drunkenly, tugging on the string.

"It flies!" she said with disbelief. "Adam, run faster. Faster!"

"You asked for it."

As he surged forward, the wind caught the kite and lifted it higher, while she tried frantically to unwind string fast enough. Tory looked forward and felt her heart plummet at the crazy speed they were building. Better to stay focused on the kite. She looked back over her shoulder.

Adam was breathing hard, and sexy little diamonds of perspiration were breaking out on his brow. Better to stay focused on the kite! She looked past his shoulder. The kite was nose-diving, straight for earth.

"Faster," she commanded recklessly.

He tried, but it was too late. The kite crashed on the hard asphalt path behind him.

"Oh, damn," she said.

Adam laughed and dug in his heels to stop them. She had to hold onto the arms of the wheelchair to keep from pitching out of it.

"Does this thing have a seatbelt?" she asked, lifting herself up and looking on the seat.

"I don't think it was ever intended to be used in quite this fashion. Put your feet down, so you don't roll away," he instructed, then went back to retrieve the kite.

She wound in the string. Adam held the kite in a straight line from her so the string wouldn't tangle.

It gave her the uncomfortable sensation of reeling in a fish.

A big fish.

A big, gloriously handsome fish.

A woman going by with a double stroller with two noisy babies in it gave Adam a smile that briefly washed the harried young mother look from her face.

Adam smiled at the babies.

Adam Reed, Catch-of-the-Day.

"Is the kite broken?" Tory called, reminding herself to keep things official. Officially they were here to fly a kite.

Never mind the way the sun looked in his hair, or how white his teeth were, or how his chest swelled, rising and falling under the fabric of his T-shirt.

"Are you kidding? A tank could run over this thing and not damage it. Which is why it's not doing so well in the air."

She had reeled him in close, and he inspected the kite, while she inspected him. Unofficially.

"It did fine," she said, too sharply. "We just need a little more speed."

"Women. Not three minutes ago you were telling me I was going too fast."

And he was. He was going way too fast. Doing things to her heart and mind that should really happen more slowly.

She made herself focus on their official business.

"If we're going to make this kite fly, you have to go *really* fast. Let's go back to the top and try again."

Adam looked up the enormous hill and sighed. "I think I liked it better before you were committed to this idea."

"I'll get out of the wheelchair. Walk up, ride down."

"Can your knee handle that?"

"Oh, sure. I can walk. I just can't run."

"Now that's a switch. You were the girl who could run but not walk."

Two teenage girls with earrings in the oddest places went by and looked at the kite, then looked at Adam, and giggled breathlessly.

"Great day for flying a kite, ladies," he said.

They giggled again, tickled by the attention.

Catch-of-the-Month, Tory thought ruefully.

He offered her his arm, and she took it, looping her own companionably through his. He pushed the empty wheelchair back up the hill, and she suddenly wondered what it would be like to grow old with him, to walk slowly, like this, through their twilight years.

She smiled to herself. As if Adam would ever slow down.

"What are you smiling about?"

"I was just thinking you will probably die at age one hundred and three in a motorcycle accident where speed was a factor."

"What made you think of that?"

She wasn't about to admit she had momentarily thought of a future together. "The wheelchair, I guess, made me think of growing old."

"You will grow old beautifully. With uncommon grace."

"Adam! No one can know these things."

"I do. I know that of you."

She could feel an embarrassing tide of red rising up her cheeks. "Well, since you can see the future so clearly, and my arriving at old age is assured, I intend to be fearless going down the hill this time."

"Good." He was looking at her with wickedness lighting his eyes. She resettled in the chair, thinking he had always done this—coaxed her wild side out. Made her bolder than she really was.

She remembered Mark watching her once, when Adam had her bent over with laughter, howling really, without any dignity at all. She had not realized it at the time, but looking back she could see something wistful in Mark's eyes.

"All right," she called, impatiently putting the memory behind her. "Go!"

They zoomed down the hill, and her fear was gone. Vanished. She cackled wild delight at the wind in her face and hair. She looked back, mesmerized for a moment by the power of him, by the easy play of muscles in his arms and legs, and then she looked over his broad shoulder.

The wind had grabbed the kite, and was tugging the string out of her fingers, begging for more.

At the bottom of the hill, Adam stopped and spun the wheelchair around with such momentum she was nearly flung out of it. But before she could give him heck for his lousy driving she saw the kite, dancing exuberantly on the wind above them.

She laughed with a pure delight that she was not sure she had felt since her childhood. The kite went up and up and up. And then without warning, it began to list.

"No! It's doing that thing, Adam."

The kite listed this way and then that, and then dipped, a big S forming in the string.

"Run," she cried.

He spun her around again and put on a heroic burst of speed, but it was too late. The kite wobbled drunkenly and then crashed to the earth.

He retrieved the kite, and she wound in the string.

"We've got a little rip here," he said. "Luckily I was given a repair kit."

He pulled a roll of masking tape from his pocket and set the kite on her lap. He bent over it, much too close for her comfort.

How she wanted to touch the springy silkiness of his hair. He smelled wonderful. Of sunshine and aftershave, and ever so enticing of sweat. All male.

A nurse went by, overweight and puffing. He glanced up at her and returned her tentative smile. She was transformed into a beauty queen before Tory's very eyes.

A half dozen more times they careened crazily down the hill. The kite was now patched in several places, and masking tape held together one of the fragile sticks that formed the kite's frame. And then, when they had both decided that keeping the kite in the air was not even a possibility, nature decided to take pity on them and the wind picked up.

The kite soared upward, pulling restlessly at the string in her hands, dancing with the wind, begging for freedom.

The string seemed to be singing off the roll in her hands. She stood up and played the string, Adam right beside her. The kite was like a living thing at the end of that tether. Pulling, soaring, falling, soaring again.

Grinning with a sense of triumph she could not explain, she finally relinquished the string to Adam, wanting him to feel what she had felt. The tug of the kite, the unexpected power of it, the beauty of its dance with the wind vibrating through his fingertips.

The kite swayed and dipped and soared like an exotic dancer making love with the wind. It nose dived and then righted itself. For twenty minutes the kite danced with the air currents.

It was an incredible thing. Beautiful.

She felt no regret at all when without warning the kite string snapped, and it was free. She laughed and waved at it as it soared yet higher, the bright dragon becoming a bright dot, and then a bright speck, in the distant sky.

"Hell's bells," Adam muttered, watching it go. "I suspect that kite just became worth a minor fortune."

"Really? How come?" She was standing in front of him and, on impulse, leaned back into the broadness of his chest.

His arms folded around her, his hands interlocked on her tummy.

They had stood like this a hundred times growing up—watching the Stampede fireworks from Scotsman Hill, at the high school football games, at the edge of the river as the sun went down.

"I rented the kite from a young entrepreneur. Very eager to make his first million. Off of me."

She felt how she had always felt in the circle of his arms. Safe. Cared about. *Right.*

"Did your young friend provide the wheelchair, too?"

"I'm afraid so. And the ricksha. And the skates."

"Him? Out-of-the-way-Gramps?"

"His name is Daniel."

"How on earth did you wind up doing business with him?" It crept into her mind, uninvited, that she was feeling something *more* than safe and cared about. There was a strange tingling beginning at the bottom of her toes and making its way stealthily toward her heart.

"I think it had nothing to do with earth, actually. In fact, it was unearthly strange how he kept popping up."

"I liked him," she said, resisting with all her might the urge to push herself deeper into the circle of his strength. "He was spunky. I think he could really go places."

"Yeah. He could, if the right opportunity came along before the wrong one."

There was something in the way he said that, that made her turn in the circle of his arms and look up at his face. It was closed.

"You're going to help him, aren't you?" she guessed.

"I already did! Rented those skates from him, the wheelchair, the ricksha. I'll be buying that blasted kite, too."

"You won't be able to leave it at that."

She felt him stiffen with surprise, before he relaxed again.

"How come you always saw in me what nobody else could see?" he asked her softly.

"Maybe, Adam, you always showed me what you never let anyone else see."

She felt good. Full. Happy. She could have easily

stayed like this forever, bigger questions not gnawing on her mind at all.

"It was fun, wasn't it?" he said, his chin resting comfortably on the top of her head.

"It was. It was a lot of fun. Better than in-line skating."

"Way better than rickshawing."

"Why do you suppose Mark picked kite flying? We never flew kites as kids, did we?"

"No. Not that I recall."

"He was right, you know. I haven't laughed enough."

"I guess I haven't really, either."

"Adam! You used to laugh all the time. What happened?"

"Work, I guess. Life. Who knows?"

"Promise me, when you go back, you'll do things that make you laugh." And there it was. The simple fact that he was going back. The reminder that what she felt in his arms was no more real than a mirage shimmering and shifting in hot desert air.

"Such as?" he asked.

"Oh, I don't know. Whinny at old ladies or something."

"You, too, then."

"What? Me whinny at old ladies?" She tried for a teasing note, but already she could feel in her heart the hurt of him going away.

"Find things that make you laugh, Tory. Promise me."

She couldn't think right now of a single thing that would ever make her laugh again. Fifty miles an hour down a hill in a wheelchair was a pretty hard act to follow. "Such as?"

"Oh, I don't know. Find some guy who'll chase you

around the bedroom and when he catches you, tickle your toes."

"Adam!"

"You still have ticklish toes, don't you?"

"I was not objecting to the ticklish toes!"

"Really? Well, then I'm going to tickle them right now, if you have no objections."

"You are not. I do have objections." *I'd rather we were in the bedroom first.* She blushed red just thinking it.

He was looking at her with wicked knowing, and she pulled out of the circle of his arms. They no longer felt safe at all. About the furthest thing from it, in fact.

"Stay away from me," she warned.

He advanced one step closer.

"Adam, I can't run. You know that."

"Yes." He twirled an imaginary moustache. "I know."

"Please, don't."

He stepped closer.

"Adam!"

"I'll trade you. I'll spare your toes in exchange for something."

"What?" she croaked, as if she didn't already know. *A kiss.* And she wanted it. She wanted him to kiss her and hold her, and tickle her toes and make her laugh. To wrestle her to the ground right here—never mind the dignified woman walking her poodle past them—and kiss her until she was absolutely breathless, until her mind couldn't think anymore about anything.

And least of all the word *forever.* How that word had betrayed her once already.

"This is the trade," he said. "You buy me a hot dog

from that little hole in the wall downtown, and I'll leave your toes alone.''

She stared at him, so deflated by that answer that she wanted to cry out in most unladylike terms exactly what he could do with his damn hot dog.

Instead she bit her lip, and tried to look at this as a reprieve from the reckless wanting inside her that would throw everything away, trade him anything, to have him tickle her toes. Preferably with his lips.

"It's not there anymore," she said of the hot dog stand.

"You must know where to get a good hot dog."

"I hate hot dogs."

"Since when?"

Since just now, when he'd wanted a hot dog and not a kiss.

"Since when?" he asked again. "He used to barbecue them, remember, and you liked yours with fried onions and mustard. No ketchup. No relish."

"Why would you remember something so silly?" she asked crossly.

"I'm a bachelor. I eat lots of hot dogs. They are not silly to me. One of the great inventions of the nineteenth century."

This is what she had to remember: he had come here because Mark had asked him to. He had not come to tickle her toes, or kiss her either, because those weren't on his stupid list.

"Give me that letter," she said, holding out her hand imperiously.

He looked at her suspiciously, then pulled it from the back pocket of his jeans.

She noticed the folds were nearly worn through. Carefully she opened it, and skimmed it quickly, not letting her heart beat harder at the part about her loving Adam better.

She folded it neatly and gave it back to him.

"Why don't we just finish this?" she suggested, surprised and pleased with the note of ice she managed to inject into her voice. "We'll drive to my parents' cabin at Sylvan Lake this afternoon. Watch the stars come out, and drive home. Then you can leave. Maybe even tonight."

Then you will be free. And so will I.

"I'll have to pay extra on the wheelchair if I don't have it back by three."

"So we'll bring it back first."

He sighed. "Okay. But I get my hot dog."

All he was worried about was hot dogs, and surcharges on that dumb chair. If it bothered him that by tonight he could be winging home, away from her, forever, that did not show.

His face was a study in indifference. But then lawyers got very good at that, didn't they? Hiding what they really felt?

She gave herself a mental shake. Why assume he was feeling anything at all? He was good at leaving the people who needed him most.

And sometime this morning, when the laughter had rippled out of her, free and flowing as a little silver mountain brook, she had become one of those who needed him most.

A fact that he was never ever going to know.

It had been a mistake, he decided, thinking about chasing her around the bedroom until she was nearly hysterical with laughter.

It had been a worse mistake saying it, even if he had

cleverly disguised his desire by putting it onto some imaginary third person.

Damn, but it was easy to imagine her collapsing on a bed, those wonderful red-gold curls scattered around her face, the laughter dying from her eyes and being replaced with a look so white-hot it could take a man's soul.

Far, far safer to switch the topic to hot dogs, not that she seemed to appreciate his clever rescue that had kept them from going to dangerous places where they could not go.

Why not? A voice within him asked. Loudly.

He dared to glance at her. Because.

She had married his best friend.

Because. He had gone on to make a life without her.

Because. The wound had never healed properly. Why rip it open again? She was absolutely right, of course.

Finish it.

And fast.

With the wheelchair loaded back into the trunk of the Viper, her silence chilly and her eyes as angry as they had been that first day, he realized they were right back where they had started. If possible a few squares behind that starting point.

Hot dogs were not "in" food in Calgary, which stubbornly made him want one more. He finally found a hot dog stand at a strip mall, but they were hot dogs at their worst—pale pink, little beads of steam and grease clinging to them.

He wolfed down three of them just to show her he hadn't even noticed how stiff and chilly she had become.

He envied the little dish of yogurt that she ordered, and tried to look back to the moment everything had changed.

From the exhilaration of that kite disappearing into no-where, to this.

His own big mouth to blame.

He'd made that awful remark about some guy chasing her around the bedroom—in his mind, of course, it had been him. And then he'd tried to make awkward amends by changing the subject to hot dogs, and she'd gone cold as ice. Could he backpedal safely to the chasing-around-the-bedroom part and take a different turn when he got there?

He studied her features. Nose tilted at the ceiling, freckles brightened from sun, hair a wild, wind-tangled sculpture that begged for his fingers to touch it.

Eyes, averted. Looking at everything but him. Reading a chart on the wall over his left shoulder. He turned and glared at it.

It showed how to properly butcher a pig, all the little sections cut away like puzzle pieces.

Why should he try and repair this terrible mess?

She was right.

Get it over with and go home. Put them both out of their misery.

The pig poster had killed his appetite for hot dogs. He could only hope not for all time.

Her mother was working in her flower bed when they stopped to pick up the key for the cabin. He wished he could just stay in the car, but good manners dictated otherwise.

Her mother made a lovely picture in her wide-brimmed straw hat, her gardening gloves on, the profusion of blooms around her as she worked her front bed. Again he was struck by the realization Tory would one day age like this—with a kind of gentle beauty. Her beauty growing with each gray hair and each crinkle around her eyes.

He reminded himself he was not going to be around to see it.

Even though he could see that hope in Mrs. Bradbury's eyes as Tory asked her for the key to the cabin.

"The cabin? Of course, though it's been closed since last year. Oh, if I'd have just known I would have gone and got it ready for you."

As if they were going there on a honeymoon, a perception Tory had not missed. Color flooded her cheeks.

"Mom, I just need to know where the lawn chairs are. We're going to look at the stars come out, and then we're coming home."

"Tory, you're an adult woman. You really don't need to tell me what you're doing. Your dad and I are always just happy when someone gets some enjoyment from the cabin."

"No one said one word about enjoyment," Tory said tersely. "The lawn chairs?"

Her mother shot him a puzzled look. He shrugged.

"Try under the back deck. Oh, look, here's the cabin key right on this chain."

Adam took the chain from her and removed the key she pointed to.

"I'll be going soon," he told her. "I probably won't see you again."

Tears swam in her eyes and made him even sorrier than he already was that he had ever come back here.

Why? Just to bring all these people pain? Tory's mother wanted him to stay and fix Tory.

Who appeared to hate him.

Tory's mother blinked back the tears, took off her gloves and hugged him hard. "You come back anytime, Adam. Anytime."

"Thanks."

From her mother's house they progressed to Daniel's. Out of the corner of his eye Adam watched Tory's reaction to the dilapidated neighborhood.

The indifference disappeared from her expression, and her brows came down as she studied the broken-down house.

"He's probably at school. I'll just drop off the—"

"There he is," she said softly.

Daniel had appeared on the porch, his hair tousled, in a wrinkled T-shirt.

Adam shook his head and got out of the car. He opened the trunk and then pulled out the wheelchair.

"I thought you were going to try school," he said, when Daniel materialized at his elbow.

"What's the point? I haven't got the money to go to university, even if I wanted to. Which I don't."

That last tacked on with an angry vehemence that spoke volumes.

Tory got out of the car, and Daniel grinned at her. "How's your leg, lady?"

Adam watched how her smile melted the hardness from Daniel's features.

"I'll be running the marathon in no time," she said lightly.

Adam glared at her. Saving all her charm for this young thug, instead of *him*.

"I lost the kite," Adam said, and braced himself for Daniel's evaluation of what the kite was worth.

"It was a beautiful kite," Tory said, absolutely beaming at the boy, who seemed to grow inches under her warm gaze. "You should have seen it fly. When it broke the string, it looked like a wild horse running free, heading right for the clouds."

"How much for the kite?" Adam asked grouchily. She

hadn't told *him* she thought the kite looked like a wild thing, freed. No sir, for him, the one who had run up and down that hill until his lungs nearly burst—the refrigerator look.

"The kite was a gift," Daniel said graciously. "For you." And he took Tory's hand, bowed over it and kissed it.

She laughed.

"Where'd you get the wheelchair?" Adam asked sternly, reminding Tory subtly they were not exactly dealing with a junior Prince Charming here.

"Says right on it," Daniel said carelessly.

"The deal was you couldn't steal it."

"I didn't steal it," he said indignantly, slipping Tory another charming little smile. "I borrowed it. I'm bringing it right back."

"You'll probably claim a reward," Adam said under his breath.

"Hadn't thought of that. Thanks, Gra—"

"Don't you dare."

"You need anything else?"

"No." But even as Adam said it, his gaze fell upon an old motorcycle on the other side of the hedge. "Is that a Harley?"

"My brother's."

Tory was watching him, for a minute something unguarded in her face. She knew that he could not walk away without having a look at it. She gave her head a small shake, but she looked pleased somehow.

Adam went through a gate that was nearly off its hinges. The bike was a beauty. Old. Exquisitely powder-coated and chromed. "Great bike," he said, an understatement. "A shovelhead. Eighty-three?"

"Eighty-four. My brother's pretty crazy about it. He's

done most of the work himself. The insurance is up next week, though, so he's riding it as much as he can this week.''

''Do you think he might like to rent it?''

Daniel's face lit up, as if he was already calculating his commission. ''If it was presented to him in the right way, he might go for it.''

''One afternoon. I'll bring it back tonight.'' *On my way to the airport.*

''I'll go talk to him.''

Daniel went up the rickety stairs and disappeared inside the house.

Tory came through the gate and looked at the bike. ''Adam, you're still crazy about these old hunks of metal!''

His lawyer's mind detected she was speaking to him reluctantly. But she was speaking to him.

''Yeah.'' *Proceed cautiously.* ''How about you?''

''I never liked motorcycles!''

''Sure you did. You used to beg me for rides, on that odd occasion that I had a bike working.''

A faint blush of pink swept her cheeks. ''I guess I did like going for rides. But that's quite different from the grand passion you always felt.''

He'd always thought his grand passion was motorcycles, too. Until this afternoon, when he'd thought about doing wicked things to her toes.

''You want to take this out to the lake? The motorcycle?''

Did she pale, the pink receding from her cheeks, too rapidly? She looked like she didn't trust herself to speak.

He was positive she was going to say no. But she didn't.

She said yes.

And he felt something warm and full of energy surge within him.

Tory could not believe this. They were standing in a yard that looked like something out of a nightmare, looking at a big black-and-silver monster of a bike, and she had just said yes to the suggestion they take it to the lake instead of that plush car he had rented.

It was madness to agree to this. Everything in her had told her to say no.

But she hadn't.

He was right. She had loved to climb on the back of the big, growling machines that he sometimes had working.

She had loved to put her arms around him, to bury her face in the aromatic leather of his jacket, to peer out past his shoulder and feel the wind in her hair and on her face.

The boy, Daniel, came back outside, his brother with him. The brother was only slightly older and had the same devil-may-care good looks as Daniel.

She could see him sizing up Adam.

She guessed that Daniel had already sized up Adam a long time ago. And in that face that tried for hardness she had seen respect and liking.

Adam had always had that. Something in him that crossed over barriers others could not.

The brother and Adam were now earnestly talking camshafts and carburetors. After they had gone over the bike in minute detail, Adam commenting and offering suggestions, a deal was arrived at, though it seemed more like a moment of kindred spirits meeting.

She realized she had agreed to ride with him. And that they were venturing now into territory far more dangerous than the laughter Mark had wanted them to discover. Now they were going backward along a road, to a place in it where they had clung together in youthful exhilaration.

But sensuality had played an enormous part during that long-ago ride.

Enormous.

She could back out. Except that she seemed powerless to do so.

Daniel brought her out a jacket and a helmet. "I'll lend these to you," he said. The jacket was black leather and had a very graphic skull and crossbones on the back. She did not think he was the kind of boy who gave things easily, and yet today he had given her a kite, and now was lending her, no strings attached, possessions he obviously cared about dearly.

Perhaps, she thought, glancing at his house, the jacket and the helmet were the most valuable things he owned.

She was so touched by his generosity she could not say no, despite the gruesome art on the back of the jacket. He held it for her, practicing being a gentleman, and again she was moved. She slipped her arms into the jacket. Daniel had not seemed that much larger than her, but he was, and the jacket swam around her. She put on the heavy helmet, and strapped it securely around her chin.

Adam, too, had been lent a jacket, his in plain black leather. When he shrugged into it, it seemed to her the years fell away from him and he became once more that wild and wonderful boy from her youth. He flashed a smile at her and she felt the bottom drop out of her belly.

He straddled the bike and glanced over his shoulder.

She joined him.

He threw his weight down on the kick start, and the

bike coughed to life, the cough melting quickly into a growl. She could feel the throb of power beneath her. Smoothly he pulled it out of the yard, bumped the motorcycle gently off the curb onto the street.

She wanted to hold on anywhere but to him.

And yet when she gave in, it felt so right.

Like coming home.

There were flowers on her kitchen table that needed drying, and there were orders that needed to be filled.

The last thing she should be doing right now was taking a ride through her past with Adam Reed.

And yet she had a sense of nothing being able to stop that which was meant to be.

And she had another sense.

Of life lived under the pervasive presence of a gray cloud, and of little streaks of sun suddenly finding their way through, piercing her soul with their brightness and their promise.

They rumbled to a stop at a light.

"You know," Adam called over the noise of the engine, "that jacket would be absolutely hideous on anyone but you."

"It is hideous!"

He laughed. "But not on you."

"Well, what is it on me?"

"Sexy."

She didn't think she had heard him correctly. "Pardon?"

"You don't say pardon when you ride a Harley," he said. "You say, 'Huh?'"

"Okay, then. Huh, what did you say?"

"I forget."

But she knew he had not forgotten. And she knew she

had heard correctly. And she felt a shiver of pure apprehension go up and down her spine.

And the sensation of light pouring through the clouds intensified.

Chapter Eight

"Adam! You are going way too fast! Adaaaam!"

And then she laughed, and he knew she didn't mean
it.

He felt he was as close to heaven as he was ever going
to get. The machine he controlled was powerful. The road
was smooth. The day was glorious.

And Tory was holding him tight.

He liked the way she rode with him, shifting her
weight exactly when he shifted his, leaning into each corner, her instincts and her balance excellent. Communi-
cation was hard because of the helmets and the roar of
the engine and the wind, and yet he felt in total com-
munication with her. He had felt the exact moment she
began to relax behind him, felt relaxation turn to contentment, and now he could feel her joy, and sensed that
she felt his.

Perhaps, between him and Tory, words were something that got in the way.

The highway to Sylvan Lake passed through the rolling farm country of south-central Alberta. They saw red barns and fat cattle, fields freshly turned and planted.

The truth was when he saw the sign that said Sylvan Lake he wanted to bypass it, to go on forever like this. To say goodbye to the world as he knew it. Toronto. The office. The routine. The profession. Everything.

To follow this road where it took them.

Forever.

A foolish word. Because the word existed, but forever itself did not. Nothing was forever. Except maybe the earth. And if he thought about it hard enough, maybe not even that.

But again he was aware of thought, his ability to analyze things nearly to death, getting in the way of feeling. Because, with her arms wrapped tight around him, he felt like anything was possible. Even forever.

He took the turnoff from Highway 2 to Highway 11X and that took them right onto Lakeshore Drive, the main road through the small town of Sylvan Lake. The summer crowds had not arrived this early in June, but he slowed the big bike to a crawl, and took in the changes. He was delighted to see many of the same old decrepit cottages stood on what must now be very valuable real estate.

The commercial district, across the street from the public beach, was changed, though, newer and glossier.

Tory pounded on his back when he tried to get by the second ice-cream parlor, and he pulled in and silenced the engine.

"How can you not stop for ice cream at a place called Mrs. Moo?" she asked him.

"It used to be a gas station, didn't it?"

She pulled off her helmet and shook her head.

Despite TV commercials that showed beautiful women taking off their motorcycle helmets and lovely hair cascading out, helmet hair was not attractive. Her hair was flattened to her head, and the shake only unstuck a piece or two.

She should have looked like a little scarecrow, but somehow she looked unbelievably lovely, in her too-large jacket with the skull on the back of it, and with her hair flattened to her head.

"I think it did used to be a gas station. Look. Thirty flavors."

He knew she would look at every single flavor carefully. She would even ooh and aah over some of the more exotic ones. And then she would pick Maple Walnut.

He took off his own helmet, gave his head a shake, and followed her through the door. The jacket really did do something for her.

Like an angel wearing a devil's garb.

It was strangely enticing. *Erotic* might be going too far. But not by much.

He watched her study the ice cream, her nose practically against the glass of the long cooler. She oohed and aahed and let the names run off the tip of her tongue as if they were delicious in themselves.

He ordered a cup of black coffee.

After twelve minutes of the most careful deliberations, she ordered Maple Walnut. It made him feel like he had never left. As if he knew her. Heart and soul.

Which, his lawyer's mind informed him, was quite a lot to read into ice-cream selection.

"You're not having ice cream?" she asked him with disbelief.

"My weakness is hot dogs and I've already had three of those today."

It was too nice to stay inside, and so they went out,

and leaned their fannies against the bike and looked out across the lake.

He sipped his hot coffee and she licked her cold ice cream, and it struck him that was how they were. Hot and cold. Opposites.

She and Mark had been more alike. Mark had liked ice cream, too. Always chocolate. Not boring, exactly, but predictable. On those rare occasions when Adam ate ice cream he always picked the one with the wildest name. Zucchini Zebra, Leopard Spotted Lemon, Pomegranate Pie.

He suddenly felt a little angry with Mark. For doing the most unpredictable thing of all. Dying. Leaving Tory alone.

Leaving him, Adam, hopelessly unqualified, to pick up the pieces.

And forcing him to recognize that somewhere in those pieces were fragments of his own heart and soul.

He glanced at Tory. She had ice cream all over her lips. With the flattened hair it should have made about the world's most unattractive picture.

Instead, he felt a sudden desire, scorching hot, to taste her ice-cream flavored lips.

A woman, twice the looker Tory would ever be, in purple Lycra shorts and a cutoff top like a bra jogged by them and smiled at him. It left him cold, though he politely smiled back. Tory was glaring up at him as if he'd answered that smile with an invitation to join them.

And the look on Tory's face heated him up.

"What?" he asked her.

"Oh! Do you always have to attract so much attention?" she asked exasperated.

He knew he could not win this one. That there was no

sense in trying. But he defended himself anyway. "It's not as if I do it on purpose."

"That's the maddening part. You're too bloody handsome for your own good."

It was spoken like an indictment, but he heard something else. Tory thought he was handsome. He supposed he had always known that Tory found him attractive. But she had never said it before. And it had not counted in the crunch, after all. It had not been enough to make her say yes to him when he had most wanted to hear it.

It made no sense at all that she would be jealous of him smiling at a woman he did not know, and did not want to know. Tory couldn't be jealous. It was not in her nature, as far as he knew. And certainly not in her nature when it came to him.

He glanced at her again. She was staring out across the lake, her facial features bland, her ice cream down to the cone.

She took an enormous bite, designed to show uncaring, but failing somehow.

His analytical mind sorted through the information and came up with an impossible answer. She had. She had experienced a moment of jealousy when he had smiled at the jogger.

Which meant something.

Something that could change his life for all time. If he let it.

The logical thing to do would be to turn around and go back right now. This road they had traveled today was bringing him face to face with yearnings he did not want to know. Dissatisfactions with his life that he had managed to keep a deep dark secret from himself for a long time.

Go back, the voice of his self-preservation called to him.

But the letter in his pocket, Mark's voice, urged him to go forward. Into the ultimate adventure of his own heart?

"Should we go, Adam?" She wiped the ice cream off her lips, missing a speck right at the corner of her mouth, and rubbed her hands on her jeans.

"Yeah, we should go." But where? Forward or back?

The cabin was both, really. A piece of the past, and a piece of the future.

He could not go back to Calgary now. Not yet. If he could hang on for another few hours, they would go and set up the lawn chairs and watch the stars come out, and then drive the motorcycle back through a star-studded night.

And then it would be over.

His obligation to Mark fulfilled to the letter, his life his own again. Simple. Uncomplicated. Predict—

He saw Tory stiffen beside him and then look sharply around.

"What?" he asked her.

"Did you hear that?"

"What?"

"I thought I heard a man laugh."

"And?"

She looked at him, her brown eyes huge. "And it sounded just like Mark."

Of course, the lawyer in him knew absolutely, beyond a shadow of a doubt, that Mark was not having a laugh at his own puny human efforts to keep everything under control.

But the boy in him, the one who had known Mark as well as he knew himself, was not so sure.

* * *

Tory rubbed a circle in the dust on the bathroom mirror and looked at herself. Her hair looked absolutely awful, flattened against her skull in the most unflattering way. She peered closer and saw there was a little smudge of ice cream at the corner of her mouth.

So his eyes straying to her mouth every now and then had meant nothing more than she needed a napkin.

The cabin seemed stuffy, damp, dark and cold. The sun would not set for another hour. The water had not been turned on yet this year, and she did not want to ask Adam to do it just so she could make herself presentable.

For him.

It was bad enough that she had felt that flare of insane jealousy when Miss Canada had jogged by them in her cute little running outfit.

Had he guessed she had experienced that moment of jealousy? Surely, at thirty years of age, she was not so transparent? Surely, at thirty years of age she was beyond petty feelings like jealousy?

"Tory," he called, "I'm going to turn on the water so that we can make hot chocolate."

"If you insist," she muttered.

She did not think agreeing to come here had been a good idea. At all. Maybe it would have been safe enough if they had stayed with the car, but that motorcycle, and the smell of leather, and being in such close physical proximity to him had woven a special kind of magic around them.

Her arms around the broad strength of him, the wind in her face, the utter freedom of it all, had made something within her sing, intensified that feeling that she was bathed in sunlight after a long sojourn through darkness.

For one heart stopping moment, when they had approached the cutoff for Sylvan Lake, she had found herself hoping he would not turn. That he would just keep going.

"To where?" she asked herself grouchily. "Edmonton? How romantic."

But even as she said it, she knew it was not about where the road would go so much as the longing in her heart that he had fanned to life. And now she had to go sit out there on a lawn chair and sip hot chocolate and watch the stars come out one by one, and pretend.

That she was not feeling confused.

That she was not feeling mixed up.

That she was not feeling jealous of every woman who looked at him and received his smile.

That she was not contemplating him leaving with a kind of dread, her heart feeling hollow every time her mind drifted to what would happen when each of the items listed in that letter had been completed.

It was as if, for five days now, her world had come into spring just as surely as the world around her was doing the same thing. All around her was new turned soil, the vibrant green of new beginning, leaves unfolding, birds singing. Hope was in the air.

And until Adam had come back, she had been comfortably unaware that she lived without hope. That her life had become dull and predictable with not even the remotest chance of an adventure coming along and setting her on her ear.

That was the way she wanted it. After losing Mark she felt an almost insane need to be in control. She went to bed at the same time every night. She ate hot oatmeal every single morning for breakfast. She didn't even like to move her furniture. She wanted to feel like there were things that would never change unless she allowed them to. She wanted so desperately for the world to be safe and predictable that she had made her own world dull and without excitement.

And then along came Adam and she practically tingled with awareness of life coursing through her veins.

Of all that was *possible*.

Of a craving within herself to flirt a tiny bit with danger. To *not* know exactly what was going to happen next.

The pipes screeched and water exploded out the tap, leaving untidy drips all over her shirt. There, she told herself. That was what happened when you didn't know what was going to happen next—a mess. A big unruly mess.

Which described her hair exactly.

She decided, firmly, that she wasn't going to fix it. Why? She could never compete with the millions of gorgeous women prepared to throw themselves at his feet anyway. Why should she fix her hair? To impress him?

To coax a few more kisses out of him, a little voice inside her informed her cheerfully.

"I do not want his kisses!" she informed the little voice back.

Liar.

"Let me put this a different way. He is leaving. Soon. Tonight, with any luck. And I am—"

"Tory, who are you talking to?"

"No one," she called, watching with dismay as her hand disobeyed her mind and reached for the hairbrush on the back of the sink.

"I'm going to go chop some wood. I think it's going to get fairly cold out here. Maybe we could have a bonfire."

Super. A bonfire. Hot chocolate. The stars coming out. And the most handsome man in the world to share it all with. Though she regretted telling him that. That she found him attractive. As if he didn't know.

After quite a long and not an entirely successful session with her hair, she joined him outside.

He was right. A chill was growing in the air, and she shivered. From the chill only. And not from the way he looked, splitting that wood.

All man. Untempered strength. The axe coming up over his head and down again in such smooth rhythm it could have been a form of ballet. Round hunks of tree trunk splitting in half with a clean snap.

He seemed to be enjoying himself—as if he had longed for something to pit his masculine brawn against. And this fit the bill perfectly. A small mountain of cleanly split wood rose on one side of him.

If he kept it up her parents would have enough wood to last them the season.

She looked at the cabin. Compared to some of the summer homes rising around this lake now, it was humble and without pretension. It was a little square box made of the formed cedar logs that had been popular a long time ago. It stood under towering pines and poplars. The front window, which she faced now, looked over the lake. There was a small porch to one side of the door, and her parents' wooden lawn chairs sat there side by side.

Looking at their chairs, she felt a sudden longing. Side by side they had sat for nearly forty years now. Her mother still looked at her dad with complete love in her eyes, and he still teased her as if she were a young girl about to blush.

Which she did often for him.

When she had married Mark, Tory had envisioned

such things. Love growing quietly. A cottage at the lake. Watching the children run down toward the water.

For a moment she could almost see them, and hear them, ghostly children running through the trees. Erupting onto the lawn. Shrieking and heading for the water. Running in. Splashing. Dashing away from one another.

Was she seeing into the future, the children she had never had? Or was she looking into the past when she and Mark and Adam had played so long and hard on the shores of this lake?

"Why so glum, chum?"

She started at the sound of his voice, and then he staggered by her and dropped an enormous load of wood at the fire pit. She noticed he already had the lawn chairs set up.

He came back toward her, smiling, just the way he used to smile all those years ago, when he had done something unforgivable, like thrown her in the water in her brand-new shorts and top, and now would charm away her anger. Smile at her and her fury would melt as though it had never been.

And this time, when he smiled, it was true. The hard ball of sadness began to melt.

"Are you thinking of him?" he asked.

"Of all of us. You and me and Mark and my mom and dad and all the years gone by."

"Me, too. The cabin seems smaller and the trees seem bigger. And there seem to be ghosts running through them, laughing."

She turned startled eyes to him, but he was looking off to the trees, a faraway look on his face.

"I never knew again moments of such wonder," he said softly. "Moments where everything felt so totally right. I seem to see our summer afternoons spent here wrapped in some kind of golden light, sparkling. The closest I've come since, is when I open up my bike and go full blast down a lonely road. And this morning. Call me crazy but I felt it this morning when you and I flew that kite.''

Again, she felt deeply startled. For that was when she had felt it, too, that golden feeling he had described. She had felt it here at the lake in the days of her childhood. She had felt it the day she had married Mark. And then again, when she and Adam had gone down that path like an out-of-control torpedo, the kite on the wind behind them.

''Look. It's getting dark. Let's see who spots the evening star first,'' he suggested.

He offered his hand, and it seemed like the most natural thing in the whole world to take it. He led her down to the lawn chair, wrapped a blanket around her, and then laid and lit the fire.

It roared to life, its sparks dancing with a sky that was turning a hue of blue that would last for only minutes before it disappeared into the darker shades of night.

''There it is!'' she called.

He turned from the fire and squinted at the sky.

Venus flickered, faded, flickered again, stronger this time.

''Make a wish,'' he told her.

She looked at him, and at how the firelight and twilight mingled and played off the ridges of his face. She looked at how tall he stood, at the pride and the confidence in the set of his shoulders.

She made her wish. A wish of such naked wanting that the heat rose in her cheeks.

A foolish wish. The kind of wish a romantic schoolgirl would make. A wish so big that somewhere the words ended and the feeling just went on and on. A feeling that had something to do with those children that had run through the trees, and something to do with toes and tickling and laughter, and something to do with believing again.

In what?

Love?

Forever?

Him? Adam Reed?

Foolish and whimsical, and yet she found herself wishing with all her heart.

The lawn chair beside her creaked as it took his weight, and she found his hand searching for hers in the blanket.

Just like that first night.

And just like that first night, when it found hers, it felt right.

"I miss him," he said quietly.

"Me, too."

Companionable silence, as the stars winked on one by one.

"Maybe he's up there, hunting with Orion," she said after a long stillness. "Do you think so?"

"I never used to think about it at all. Now I do all the time."

"And?"

"I don't know, Tory. My brain says when it's over, it's over. They put you in the ground and you turn to dust."

"But?"

"But my heart says my brain is the stupidest part of my body."

She laughed softly.

"Tory, my heart says he's with us. In the people we

became because we had the privilege of knowing him. But it's more, even than that. It's like he's here, somehow, looking out for us. Loving us still. Like the love goes on.''

"Like that old-fashioned saying. Love abides.''

"Exactly.'' He got up suddenly, as if he had made himself uncomfortable. "I'm going to make that hot chocolate.''

"All right.'' She sat there in the deepening darkness, watching lights wink on across the lake at Jarvis Bay. She tilted back her head and looked at the stars. They seemed extra special tonight. Like they were dancing and laughing. As if they knew the secrets of the universe and could not contain their joy at knowing them.

He came back, silently, coming out of the night, and yet she knew as soon as he drew closer. It was as though the air around her were charged with his presence.

He pressed the hot chocolate into her hands and took the seat next to her.

"I'm glad I'm here,'' he said. "I don't make time anymore to just sit and feel the world. You do. You feel it through your flowers and the creations you make.''

She had not thought of it that way, but she knew it was true. Working closely with the bounty of nature, utilizing her creative spirit, had brought her the only contentment she had known in the last year.

He added more wood to the fire and the sparks leapt and danced.

She felt as if she could stay like this forever.

And then he reminded her about that word.

"We're going to have to go soon, Tory. It's getting really cold, and I don't want you to turn into a popsicle on the back of that bike.''

It felt as if nothing could take the warmth from her,

but as soon as she reluctantly crawled out from under the blanket, she knew that was not the case. He looked after dousing the fire while she went to the cabin and rinsed the mugs.

"You can leave the water on now," she called to him, "it's not likely to freeze in June. Even if this is Alberta."

"Don't be too sure," he said, and came in letting the screen door slap shut behind him. "It is really cold out there. And not much better in here."

By flashlight they locked the cabin and made their way through the filtered light of the moon to where the bike sat.

She thought of the wish she had made. Not about to come true.

And she thought, suddenly, of the last time they had ridden through the darkness together on his motorcycle.

It had ended in a proposal of marriage.

That she had turned down. She sighed, and he looked at her sharply, then did up the zipper on his jacket.

Over, she thought.

It was over.

It was over, he thought, as he did up his jacket. He took one more look at the star-studded night and tried to quell the feeling of regret welling up inside of him.

His contract fulfilled. His obligation over.

She stood by the bike, and he remembered a long time ago when they had stood by a bike together in the darkness.

It had been a crazy night.

He had been working on the motorcycle, and at four in the morning, by some strange miracle, it had growled to life. The exhilaration he had felt in that moment simply could not be borne alone. So he had gone next door and tapped on her bedroom window and she had come to it, looking sleepy and pleased and not at all annoyed, even though the first thing she told him was that she had university classes in the morning.

Never mind that, he'd told her. He'd promised her a night of magic, and it had been easy to talk her into it.

Out her bedroom window she had come, giggling, loving the excitement, the adventure, loving being bad for once.

They had gotten on the bike and headed toward Banff, the Rocky Mountains huge dark mammoths in the distance. Predawn changed them to gray, and then the first faint blush of pink touched their tops. It was then that he pulled off the road, and they had sat silently and watched. An elk, ghostly and majestic, moved silently across the road in front of them.

He had never felt, before or since, the utter sense of rightness he had felt in that moment. Totally at one with the universe. The highway, the bike, the mountain, the elk, the dawn.

And her.

The person he loved best in the world sharing it with him.

And he had known then, that he had wanted it for all time. Her beside him for each of these moments that life offered.

And so, he had asked her to marry him.

And he had seen a flare of joy in her face so strong that for a moment he had believed. And then that was gone. A trick of light perhaps. And she had looked suddenly frightened and unsure, and the moment had been destroyed utterly.

They had not even gone on to Banff.

She had told him, with tears standing out in her eyes,

and her hand resting on his arm, that no, she could not marry him.

Absolutely not, no.

And not long after that she and Mark had announced their engagement.

"You're thinking of it, too," he said suddenly, "aren't you?"

She took a startled step back from him, looked carefully at her toes, and then at the snap on her leather jacket. "Thinking of what?"

He stepped into her space. She had never been able to fool him.

"That night we went to Banff. Almost to Banff."

He saw the tears glitter in her eyes.

"Yes." *Leave it,* the part of him that was a gentleman instructed. *Leave it. Can't you see you're upsetting her?*

But the part of him that was a pure rogue could not leave it.

"Why?" he asked.

"Adam, please don't."

"Didn't you love me?"

"You know I did!"

"Didn't you love me as much as him?"

"That's an unfair question."

"I need to know."

"Adam—"

"Please." He heard the pleading in his own voice, and was ashamed of it.

"It wasn't about you, Adam, or about Mark either. It was about me."

"I don't understand."

"I could have never made you happy."

"You couldn't have *made* me happy?"

"No."

"Since when had I ever asked you to make me happy? People don't make each other happy."

"Let me word this another way. You would not have been happy with me."

"How can you say that?"

"Adam, I'm boring. I have always been boring. I probably always will be."

He stared at her. "You? Boring?"

"You asked me on an impulse. You hadn't thought it through. At all."

"I never thought of anything else. Not since I was twelve years old."

"You were probably feeling all hot and sexy and thinking if I said yes we could just progress to the nearest motel."

"I never thought of you as a motel kind of girl," he said grimly. Though he couldn't deny the rest of it. He'd been twenty-two years old. He'd thought of sex all of the time.

"Adam, I am trying to tell you I am the most ordinary of women."

"You're not!"

"Yes, I am."

They were arguing. He realized they were standing out here in the dark arguing over things that were over and done with. It served no purpose at all—all it did was make the blood drain from her face and the freckles stand out on her nose.

He wanted to shake her. Victoria Bradbury ordinary!

Victoria Mitchell, he reminded himself.

"Get on the damn bike," he said.

She did, her nose stuck in the air.

He thrust his weight down on the kick start with savage strength. He couldn't wait to leave her behind forever.

To get on that plane for Toronto and forget he had ever met this aggravating, annoying, frustrating, galling woman!

His energetic jump on the kick starter was rewarded with a strange, hollow thunking sound. Nothing more.

He drove his leg down on the kick start again, and again heard only the empty clunk. He looked up at the stars. And it was his turn to think he heard Mark laughing.

Chapter Nine

Adam watched Tory cross the driveway and go up the steps to the cabin. Her nose was still pointed toward the stars and her hips were swishing. She unlocked the door and went in and the screen slapped closed behind her.

He turned the flashlight on the bike.

The truth was this kind of problem was something of a relief.

He knew motorcycles and he knew how to fix them.

For the first time in five days he was entering his comfort zone. Problems were his specialty. You pitted your experience and intellect against them and you solved them.

Legal problems. Mechanical problems.

Now those other kind—like the kind that had just sashayed into the house—those were utterly baffling to him.

Problems that dealt with feelings were untidy things. Not cut-and-dried and neat at all.

A little whistle on his lips, he found the bike's tool kit,

strung the flashlight from a tree branch so it illuminated his work area, and went to it.

It was freezing in the cabin. Through the screen door Tory could hear him whistling. "Jingle Bells." An appropriate choice since it felt as if it might start snowing at any minute.

He actually seemed happy to be out there taking that motorbike to pieces.

Which made her furious with him. How could he bring up that awful night, and then dismiss it at the first clunk of a mechanical problem.

She went out the back door to his freshly cut woodpile and loaded up. She dumped the load in front of the wood stove in the cabin, and crumpled up newspaper with far more force than was necessary. She added kindling and struck a match.

Actually, that night had not been awful. It had been absolute magic. She had felt as if she could reach up and touch the stars that had shone in the sky above them. She had felt like they were explorers of the universe, hurtling through space. She had felt an extraordinary kinship with him, though not one word had passed between them since he had hauled her out her bedroom window.

She had felt as if she could *feel* his spirit soaring, kicking up its heels like a colt let out on a green pasture. His confidence about himself and about life showed in the effortless way he controlled the powerful machine.

In university once, in a class whose name she had long since forgotten, the professor had talked about peak experiences—called that because that was what mountain climbers felt when they reached the peak they had struggled toward.

And she would look back on that night always as that. A peak experience.

The part when he had asked her to marry him was the most exhilarating of all—like pulling incredibly clean, pure air into her lungs from the very top of the world. Like standing on the edge of a cliff, hurtling herself off and making the splendid discovery she could fly.

For that moment she had felt joy such as she had never known it.

Even now she could picture him exactly. Moonlight dancing off dark hair, his broad shoulders relaxed under the dark leather of his jacket, faded jeans hugging muscular thighs. She could see his eyes, dark and enigmatic, focused so intently on her it still could make her shiver all these years later.

She had looked at his hands, powerful and well-shaped, and for a moment allowed herself to think what marrying him would actually mean. The things they could do together. The places those hands would go.

She had accused him, just a few minutes ago, of being motivated in his proposal by feeling hot and sexy. Maybe he hadn't felt those things at all that night. Maybe it had been just her. She had read the expression "swooning" in books, and had thought it was absolute nonsense, the domain of weak-witted ninnies.

But that night, looking at him, wanting him, feeling a primal fire burning within her, she had come very close. To swooning.

Maybe it was that very loss of her customary control that had brought her back to her senses. And made her look beyond the glory of Adam in moonlight. Adam was impulsive. Much of his charm came from the ability to give himself, with complete spontaneity, to what any given moment offered. He was a guy who could turn a trip to the grocery store for milk into a laughter-filled adventure. He was the guy who could make dullest moments bright.

He did what felt good in the moment, and in that moment, with no more thought than he had given to jumping his bicycle over a cliff, he had asked her to marry him.

Thinking perhaps to capture the magic of the night for all time. If it had been another girl riding behind him, would he have asked her, too? Who knew what he had thought?

She only knew after that flash of joy, after that struggle to douse the flames of passion that threatened her to her soul, came doubt after doubt after doubt.

Her parents were her models of how to behave, and as far as she could tell, they had never done anything impulsively.

But tonight he had said he had wanted nothing else since he was twelve. That it had not been an impulse at all.

And at dinner the other night, it had been embarrassingly obvious that her parents would have no objection now if she married Adam.

She suspected it might have been a different story back then.

Tory snorted, and shoved a larger log onto the licking flame. As if anybody started planning who they would marry when they were twelve. And yet she could not bring herself to call him a liar, because that was one thing Adam had never, ever been.

Besides, in the end it had not been his character that had made the decision for her, but her own.

What she had said to him tonight was the absolute truth: she saw herself as an ordinary girl back then, not up to the challenges of leading a life of excitement and high adventure.

She had thought he would travel the world and climb the Himalayas. She had thought he might ride the high plains on half-broken horses. She had thought he would learn to surf in the warm waters of Hawaii and learn to speak Spanish. In Spain. She had thought he would consult on oil-well fires or travel to the Far East to learn Buddhism from the Dalai Lama.

She had thought he would lead a life that did not have room for someone like her. Someone who would stifle him. Who would be afraid to bungee-jump from the bridge or trek through the jungle. Someone who had to eat at eight and noon and seven. Someone who liked clean sheets and the same bed.

She had wanted stability.

And Adam had not seemed like the one who could give it to her.

The quiet love she had for Mark had seemed like the lasting kind, so close to the kind of love her parents had enjoyed for so many years. The kind that would help her raise children. The kind that would see them growing old together side by side in their rocking chairs.

Outside, a wrench hit the ground with a clatter.

Not on their motorcycles!

The fire blazed, and she felt suddenly tired. Worn out completely from the constant demands on her emotions that the last five days had made.

When she went to find a place to lay down her weary head, she found the rest of the cabin was still unbearably cold, so she tugged a mattress off a bed and brought it in front of the fire. She searched the cabin, but found only the one blanket that she had been wrapped in outside, and so she laid it on the mattress and crawled underneath it.

She closed her eyes and willed herself to go to sleep.

Instead she thought of that letter Mark had sent Adam.

It hurt her that Mark had thought she loved Adam better than him.

Differently, she defended herself. Not better, but differently.

She heard a long string of curse words from outside and could not help but smile.

And then, suddenly, without warning, she knew the truth.

Not differently.

She had loved Adam better. Always.

The tears gathered behind her eyes, and spilled down her cheeks, as she contemplated this betrayal and the fact that Mark had known.

She had loved Adam better, and been afraid of the intensity of that love. Been afraid of the mountain tops Adam brought her to. Been afraid of falling from such dizzying heights.

What did any of it matter now?

He was leaving.

If it weren't for that stupid bike out there, he'd almost be gone.

Why look at the past?

And then she knew. She had to look at it before she could move on, before she could have a future.

She had to acknowledge this wild and reckless side of herself that was so much like Adam's. Her repressed side.

The side of her that had wanted to say yes—to mountain climbing and bronc riding and exploring the whole world with a knapsack on her back. The part of her that had said yes, once, to that spontaneous motorcycle ride at four in the morning. And known then, with fear and exhilaration, that the world as she knew it was limited, and that he could open it up for her beyond her wildest dreams.

The tears still wet on her cheeks, she thought again of that letter. *She knows a little more about the nature of life, now. She won't be afraid to take what it offers her.*

But she was.

Not, she reminded herself, that it had offered her anything.

Adam had fulfilled his *obligation* to her. And offered her nothing beyond that. Except a little glimpse of her own soul.

And his. How could he have wanted nothing else but to marry her since he was twelve?

An hour passed, and sleep did not come. She put more wood on the fire and listened to him alternate between whistling ''Jingle Bells'' and cussing. She suspected he was in his element.

Another hour passed, and she dozed and woke, and dozed and woke.

When she woke again, he was standing in the doorway, rubbing his hands together, blowing on them. She could see he was shivering, and then she heard the rain falling on the roof of the cabin.

''Is the motorcycle fixed?'' she asked sleepily.

''No.''

He came over to her, and looked down, and smiled.

He had a streak of grease across his cheek, and in that smile was something so intimate and unguarded that it felt like it would keep her warm forever.

''Come to bed, Adam,'' she said. ''We'll think of it in the morning.''

He stiffened, and looked around. "Bed? You mean with you?"

She laughed softly. "This is the only blanket. And the only fire. And you look frozen."

"I hope you know what you're doing," he growled.

"I'm going to sleep," she told him sternly. "And so are you."

He glared down at her.

Her heart beat wildly. She really was playing with fire. And a part of her wanted this. To torment him. To drive him over the edge of his control. To own him physically. And even while a part of her wanted it so badly it felt as though her heart had stopped in her chest, her spirit told her no. That she could never have Adam in that way. To have him physically *only* would never soothe that part of her soul that craved to have him completely.

That part of her that had craved him since she was twelve years old.

She closed her eyes against the utter temptation of him. Closed her eyes against the way he stood, so strong, so sure, so big, so male. Closed her eyes against the slow fire that burned in his own eyes.

He stomped off and a minute later she heard water running.

And then he was back, his chest naked, his damp jeans clinging to the hard muscles of his legs.

Even she was not going to tempt fate to the extent of telling him to take those pants off.

He folded back the blanket and slid under the cover.

She could feel the warmth of his skin, though he did not touch her. He smelled of rain and motors, and it was intoxicating.

His chest was broader and deeper than she remembered it being all those years ago, each muscle exquisitely carved. His skin looked like bronze in the firelight and begged the touch of her fingers. She curled them into fists at her sides.

"What's wrong with the motorcycle?" she whispered.

"Damned if I know."

She heard the hoarseness in his voice and knew he wanted to touch her, and the heady sensation of power almost overruled her deeply felt sense that she could not, ever, have him in just this way, and survive it.

"When did it start raining?" she asked, trying to create a casual conversation that would get her head working harder than her hormones.

"About an hour ago."

Terse. Uncooperative.

And then she knew. She did not know if it would ever be possible to have Adam the way she desired him: heart, soul, mind. Body. But she knew that something between them was broken, and that she had to do her part to fix it.

She doubted that words could ever be enough, and yet she knew they had to be said. "Adam?"

"Yeah?"

"I'm sorry. I'm sorry I hurt you."

She dared not look at him. And she dared not try to fill the yawning silence with all the nervous words that came to her mind.

"You did the right thing. You married the right guy." His voice was gruff with emotion.

"I'm sorry I accused you of asking me on an impulse. And I'm sorry I accused you of having an ulterior motive. It was wrong for me to suggest you planned to end the evening in a motel, when you never treated me with anything but absolute respect in all the time I knew you."

Silence.

She took a deep breath, and finished, her voice shaking. "I was so incredibly and richly blessed to have two such remarkable men love me."

"Tory, be quiet."

She would have done anything to erase the tremendous pain from his voice, but she knew it was not in her power to erase it. They lay side by side, stiff, not touching, the tension coiled between them like a snake.

She knew, all this time, all these days of flying kites, and laughing, and behaving foolishly, all of that was for this.

For this moment when a bridge could be built across the pain. The pain of a strong love gone wrong, somehow by taking an unplanned turn on the road of destiny.

Through the darkness she could feel his struggle. And then he sighed. "Come here," he commanded softly.

And she did, willingly. She went into his arms as though she belonged there. She melted into him, clung to him as though he were a life raft in a storm-tossed sea, as though he were a huge oak, untouched by the ravages of the wind, as though he were a rock in an ocean of shifting sand.

He did not try to kiss her, but held her tight against his body.

It was hot and muscular and beautiful, and if he would have done one thing to invite her, she would have explored every square inch of it with her tongue.

But he did not.

Instead the finely held tension seemed to leave him. His breathing grew steady and deep.

He kissed her, once, on the top of her head, and then he slept.

In the morning when she woke, the place beside her was empty. Watery sunshine was streaming in the window, and a freshly laid fire crackled. She could smell coffee and hear the deep rumble of the motorcycle engine.

Adam stared at the motorcycle, absolutely baffled. When he had tried to start it last night, one last time in the pouring rain, nothing. He had given up and gone in. And now, without his having done a single thing, the big machine purred in front of him as if it had never stopped.

He shut it off and restarted it to see if it was a fluke. It wasn't.

He shook his head. Now things were reversed. The machine was baffling him, and his emotions were not.

Something very important had happened last night.

He had gone in and she had been sleeping on that mattress by the fire. He had stopped and looked down at her, her face awash in the gentle glow of the fire, and thought she looked young again. As if life had never touched her face with tragedy at all. Had his mission succeeded then?

He'd not been very happy about her invitation to sleep with her. To share the bed and the blanket, but not any of the usual things a man and a woman of their ages and experiences *should* be sharing. It seemed to him that anyone should be able to see that would be the perfect solution to the chill that rocked him.

He wondered what she looked like naked, and the chill disappeared, just like that.

He had gone to the bathroom and cleaned up, amazed by how that streak of grease across his cheek washed the years from his face as surely as the muted light of the fire had washed them from hers.

And while he contemplated his reflection and flinched from the icy cold water coming out of the taps, it oc-

curred to him that her asking him to share the mattress
with her said something that he had wanted to know for
a long time.

She trusted him.

Perhaps that was more important, slightly, than a
night's ecstasy in her arms.

How could one have just a single night with her, anyway? It would make everything impossibly complicated.

It would make getting on that plane for Toronto in-
conceivable.

No, sleeping with Tory, really *sleeping* with her, as in
chasing her around the bedroom and tickling her toes and
other places, would have to involve some deep thought.
About things like commitment.

Even as a boy he had known that to follow the breathless sensation she caused in him to its natural conclusion
would mean giving serious thought to serious questions.

Like what he was doing with the rest of his life.

And what she was doing with the rest of hers.

It seemed he had always known the answers, though,
even before he had been able to fully articulate the questions.

He had not lied to her tonight. At twelve years old he
had committed to her. Completely. Never veering from
his path. Never wanting anyone else. Never even exploring the possibility of life without her.

He'd just saved the actual question until shortly before
his twenty-third birthday.

It occurred to him it would destroy him to be rejected
by her twice. Destroy some little flame that leapt eternally
hopeful within him.

And really, while he was dead tired, stranded, soaked
in Sylvan Lake, it was hardly the ideal time to contem-
plate such weighty matters.

Knowing he didn't have a hope of going to sleep, despite a weariness that went clear through to his bones, he had gone back in there and lain down beside her.

She smelled sweet. Her lemon scent mixed with wood smoke. It was intoxicating. He wanted to cuddle up to her, but his jeans were wet and he didn't want her to be cold.

And something in him held back from her. Something vulnerable.

And then she had said it.

That she was sorry she had hurt him all those years ago on a star-studded night on the road to Banff when he had finally shared with her his heart's desire.

He had not thought his proposal would be such a surprise to her. He had thought, somehow, that she knew how he felt, and that she had felt it, too.

Her rejection had utterly crushed him.

He had thought what they had done to one another could not be fixed, and so he was astounded at how those simple words she had spoken tonight reached into his heart, right past the scar tissue. Some ache, hardly acknowledged, and yet gnawing inside him for seven years, was suddenly dead center of his awareness.

He could tell by the way she spoke the words, she really was sorry. When he snuck a look at her, her face only inches from his, he could see little white salt trails down her cheeks where the tears had flowed.

And he realized he had never forgiven her, and he did it in that instant. Forgave her completely for hurting him.

In the sensation of freedom that he felt, he realized that something within himself had been coiled tighter than a cobra ready to strike for far too long. And he wondered why he was really back here. Had it really been to make her smile, or had it been for this moment right here and right now?

Had it been to heal her heart, or his own?

His whole thought process seemed relaxed and pure and filled with incredible clarity.

And because of that, in those moments before he slept, he knew what Victoria's secret really was.

All those years he had thought that it was that she loved Mark better, and it was not that at all.

He knew why he had gone away and stayed away. He looked at himself with this new self-knowledge and liked what he saw.

A man who had managed, through incredible odds, to be loyal to both his best friends.

He felt the sweet warmth of her, cuddled in his arms, and knew a great and surging joy. He did not know what the future would hold.

This moment was enough.

Adam seemed different this morning, Tory thought, watching him. Boyish and happy. As if a weight had been lifted from his shoulders.

"You really should have picked a career that had something to do with motorcycles," she told him.

He grinned at her.

The way he was looking at her made her want to shout from mountain tops—pure exhilaration in his dark eyes, as if the years had rolled back, and they were young again, the best of friends, no hard lessons of life between them.

She had to drop her eyes from his, because his expression made her so happy, and so afraid.

"Are you going home today?" she asked him, thinking an answer would help her choose between the joy and the fear.

"I don't know," he said, his eyes locked on her, as if it all depended on her. He climbed onto the bike and it roared to life.

"How did you fix it?" she called.

He shook his head and shrugged as if he had not worked his own particular brand of magic on it.

She climbed on behind him, and rested her cheek against the back of his shoulder. She wished she could make this trip last forever.

There was that word again. *Forever.*

And somehow both her joy and her fear were connected to that word. And to him. The morning was wet and smelled good. Everything looked washed clean. It seemed the trip home did not take nearly the same amount of time as the trip there. Was that only because she wanted it to last and last—swooping through time with him?

He dropped her in front of her house and waved.

He did not say when he would see her again.

If ever.

Her heart plummeted at the thought.

She went into her house and all the things that had looked so familiar to her only yesterday—that had given her comfort and joy—seemed meaningless. Without any substance at all, let alone the power to give joy.

Her message machine was blinking, and she listened to it. Orders for flower arrangements. Questions about flower arrangements that were overdue.

Her mother's voice asking about her trip to the cabin.

And suddenly she knew she needed to talk to her mother.

* * *

Her mother poured her coffee and then went to her kitchen counter and arranged fresh-cut blossoms, little water droplets clinging to the petals, in a vase.

"How was the cabin?" she asked over her shoulder.

Trying, Tory noticed, not to appear too interested.

"It was okay."

"What did you do there?"

"Watched the stars come out. You know."

"I don't know," her mother said, raising an eyebrow at her.

"Not that," Tory said, blushing. "Really, mother."

"Well, I phoned you late last night. And you weren't home yet. I just wondered."

"The motorcycle broke down. We ended up staying the night. *Mother!*"

"I didn't say anything!" She came over to the table, put the flowers down and sank into the chair across from Tory.

"As if you had to. Good grief. Isn't there a law that says mothers aren't supposed to wish *that* for their daughters until after marriage?"

"Marriage?" her mother said eagerly.

Tory was silent, and then after toying with her coffee cup for a long time she looked up at her mother and asked the question she had come here to ask.

"How would you have felt if I'd married Adam instead of Mark?"

"I was always surprised you didn't," her mother said softly.

Tory's mouth fell open.

"Oh, darling, not that I doubted you loved Mark, it's just that you and Adam had something so very special. A spark that most people search for all their lives and never, ever find."

"Mark knew," Tory whispered.

"Yes. I think he did."

"Oh, God."

"We all knew, Tory. I think everybody knew but Adam. That you loved him best."

"It scared me loving him so much."

"I know, sweetheart."

"He was so wild."

"What you wanted most to be," her mother said softly.

"I did love Mark. I never lied to him."

"There are as many kinds of love as there are flowers in my garden, Tory. And the kind you had with Mark was good. It was strong and loyal and loving. But you would not be betraying him if you chose a different kind now. I think it is what he would want for you."

"Oh, Mom, Adam doesn't—"

"Have you asked him?"

"He's supposed to ask me!"

"He already did once, dear."

"How do you know?"

"A mother knows some things. She just knows. Tory, don't expect him to lay his heart at your feet again. Not unless you have made it very clear how you are feeling. Have you?"

"Of course not. I've been hiding it from him."

"Darling?"

"Yes, Mom?"

"Don't. Don't hide what you are feeling from him."

"I should tell him?" she whispered.

"Trust him," her mother said.

"I'm scared."

"So, go back to your little house and make flower arrangements and never know."

"I have to know."

"Life is offering you something wonderful, Tory. But you have to have the courage to take it."

Tory realized she had taken a different path once because she was too afraid to grab life with both hands.

Mark had said she knew a little more about the nature of life now, that she wouldn't be afraid.

And suddenly she wasn't.

She knew where Adam was staying. Was he still there? Or had he already gone? He would say good-bye to her, surely?

Or would he?

She left her mother's place and debated going back to hers for her car, but suddenly she just wanted to run.

Partway there, she realized she was still in her rumpled clothes from last night.

Who knew what lewd conclusions the mother she had always considered so prim and proper had entertained about that?

It occurred to her that her hair was still flattened from the helmet.

It occurred to her that she was starting to sweat.

When she asked for his room number at the hotel she reacted to the clerk's look of superiority with a grin.

He was still there.

And Adam never seemed to care what she looked like.

Adam had always seen her heart.

She was going to tell him.

Flat out.

That she loved him. Madly. Wildly. Always.

She was going to fling herself into his arms, and ask him to marry him. She was going to—

She knocked on the door of his room, noticing that the surroundings were absolutely posh.

For her. She suspected that all he had become was for her.

The door opened.

The most beautiful woman she had ever seen stood there. Her hair was glossy black and her eyes sapphire-blue. She was wearing clothes that were fresh and un-rumpled and screamed designer label. She was tall and slender and strong looking. A woman suited for any kind of adventure.

She was Adam's amazon.

And the message Tory had come to give him died in her throat.

Instead, she felt shame at her own arrogance. She had assumed Adam did not love this woman. How could he not love such a woman as this exotic beauty who stood before her? She had assumed because his motorcycle wasn't a two-seater, his girlfriend didn't ride with him.

This woman would ride her own bike. Right beside him. Not behind him.

"Yes?" the woman asked, amused eyes taking in Tory's appearance.

Tory could hear a shower pounding behind her.

"Wrong room," she whispered, and turned away before the tears that pricked her eyes could fall.

Chapter Ten

"Adam, a girl came to the door while you were in the shower. A woman, really, though there was something delightfully girlish about her. She said she had the wrong room, but I just had the feeling—"

Adam froze, the towel to his head.

Tory.

"What did she look like?" he asked carefully.

"Short hair. Copper curls. Puppy dog eyes."

He muttered a word that always made Tory laugh. Kathleen frowned.

"Adam?"

"Kathleen, I have to tell you the whole story."

"And I have one to tell you. That's why I came. Should we do it over lunch?"

What he wanted to do was chase out the door after Tory. But he knew he had loose ends to tie up here first. It had been a shock to come back to his hotel and find Kathleen waiting for him, but he had known it was an opportunity.

It would be unforgivable for Kathleen to feel they had any future at all.

But he'd still had grease on him that the cold water at the cabin hadn't been able to strip off, and he badly needed a few minutes to himself to think over what he would say. He'd taken a shower.

Why had Tory come here?

It made some hope begin to pound so hard in his chest he could barely hear what Kathleen was saying as they had lunch in the hotel restaurant.

But he did hear it. Something about an old boyfriend from college dropping by unexpectedly, and them getting reacquainted, and it being absolutely magic.

"You and I never had magic, Adam," she said ruefully. "As much as that's what I wanted for us, I just couldn't make it happen."

He swung around at the sound, scanning the room.

"What?" she asked. "Good grief, Adam, you look like you've seen a ghost."

"Not seen one," he muttered, "but certainly heard one laugh."

"Tell me about the girl," she said, a smile in her eyes. "Adam, you look different from how you looked a few days ago. Younger. No, not younger exactly. I can't put my finger on it."

So he told her about the letter. And Mark. And Tory.

"You love her," Kathleen said with soft reverence. "That's what I see in your face that I've never seen there before."

Adam said nothing.

"What are you going to do about it?"

When Adam said nothing, Kathleen laughed. "Oh, Adam, you're just like your dad. Remember when Hanna took an interest in him and we couldn't believe how he resisted her even though you and I and the rest of the world could see how right it was?''

"I remember."

"Does it run in the family?"

"Maybe."

"You have to go to Tory and tell her what you feel. What you've always felt."

"I already did that once."

"Adam, are you scared? You?"

"I'm invoking privilege. Terrified."

Kathleen covered his hand with hers. "I saw something in her eyes when I opened the door today."

"What did you see?"

"That you have absolutely nothing to be afraid of."

An hour later he put Kathleen in a cab, kissed her lightly on the forehead good-bye, and wished her well from the bottom of his heart. He glanced around. The flower girl was not on her usual corner and for a moment he was afraid he would have to get them somewhere else.

And then he saw her, darting in and out of the pedestrian traffic, her face lighting up when she saw him, her basket full of flowers.

"I need something from you," he told her, and when he told her what her mouth fell open, and then her eyes filled up with tears.

"That will pay my rent for a month. You're not just doing it for me, are you? You really need them, don't you?"

"I really need them."

"You could get them cheaper somewhere else."

"I know."

"You're a good man," she whispered.

"I hope so."

"I hope she deserves you."

He smiled. "She does."

Tory lay on her couch. She still had not changed out of the rumpled clothes. A half gallon of Maple Walnut ice cream melted in its bucket on the floor beside her, the spoon sticking in it forlornly.

It was too early to be eating ice cream.

In quantity.

She had the TV on, too.

The soaps. She had never watched an entire soap opera in her life, but she was taking pleasure in the pain and angst and complicated relationships being played out before her eyes.

She hiccupped from crying and blew her nose.

She would not even look in the mirror.

The doorbell rang and she ignored it.

It rang again. And again.

And that was followed by what sounded like a savage kick to her beautiful door.

Break in, she told the intruder, silently. Kill me. I'm ready to go.

"Hey, lady, open up."

Did she recognize that voice? Reluctantly, she went to her living room window and flipped back the curtain. Daniel stood out on her porch. He waved at her.

She closed the curtain.

God, she looked like something the cat had dragged in. She wasn't opening the door.

"Come on, Mrs. Mitchell!"

She looked back out at him. When had he come to know her name?

"My whole future is riding on this," he called.

Sighing, she padded to the door and opened it a crack.

"Look," he said, stood back, and bowed dramatically toward the road.

Over his shoulder, parked at the curb, was his ricksha. The passenger compartment was crammed full to overflowing with flowers. The bright blossoms were shoved in from floor to roof. There was a trail of them on the road.

"I felt like an idiot driving that thing down the street," he said, grinning.

She stared at him, and at the flowers, and back at him.

"Gramps plays for high stakes. He said he'd get me a scholarship. He thinks I'd make one hell of a lawyer. Me."

For a moment, her own pain seemed to fade, and she could see the happiness, the hope, in Daniel's face.

"You would make a good lawyer," she told him.

"Ha. I mean my family has been on the other side of the law for as long as I can remember. Me, a lawyer?"

"I can see it."

He beamed. "Do you know how much a good lawyer can make?"

"Ah, no, I guess I don't."

He told her.

"A day?" she asked him.

He laughed. "An hour!"

"So, is your scholarship contingent on the delivery of this contraption full of flowers?" she asked, dazed.

"I'll probably talk just like you in a year or two," he said happily. "I think he's getting me a scholarship because he's taken a liking to me, but I kind of felt obliged to help him out after that, you know?"

"I don't think I do. What exactly are they for? The flowers?"

"Lady! For you!"

"Oh." Of course. The grand gesture. Good-bye with a flair. Making himself unforgettable, as if he was not that already. "So, he's gone?"

She had to know.

"Gone?"

"Back?"

"Back where?" Daniel asked baffled.

"Home. To Toronto."

Daniel shook his head. "He's gone all right. Back. Right over your back fence."

She stared at him in horror. Her hand flew to her hair.

"You got that right," Daniel said. "A mess. And white stuff on your lip. Right here." He touched the corner of his own lip.

"Oh, my God." She slammed the door in his face.

"What am I supposed to do with the flowers?" he yelled.

She didn't know where to go first. She ran into the bathroom. It would be hopeless trying to fix her hair. She ran into her bedroom. She had to change. She had to—

"Torrrry!"

She froze. It was the cry of a man in pain. She peered out her bedroom window. Adam was lying on top of a completely flattened mugho pine holding his leg and moaning.

She went out the back door at a dead run. "What have you done?" she asked, coming to her knees beside him.

His hair was over his eyes. She gave in, and brushed it back with her fingertips.

"Sorry," he said, gazing up at her. "I don't think the other tree is going to make it either. I'll replace them."

"I meant, to you."

"I seem to have twisted my ankle. I think we're really too old for this, Tory."

"Too old for what?"

"You know."

"I'm afraid I don't."

"Why did you come to my hotel?"

"I forgot my wallet. On the bike. It didn't matter. It didn't have any money in it."

"I never saw it," he said suspiciously. "How can you forget something on a motorcycle?"

"Are you calling me a liar?"

"Yes."

"Oh."

"So?"

"So what?"

"Why did you come to my hotel room?"

"I wanted to meet your girlfriend. Whom you are seeing. She's very lovely."

"Could you help me up?"

She didn't want to touch him again. She was afraid what little resolve she had would dissolve like sugar in hot water. She helped him up.

He leaned heavily on her, and limped slowly toward her house.

"Why did you come to my hotel room?" he asked once she had him settled at her outside patio table.

"Would you like coffee?"

"Not particularly. She's not my girlfriend anymore."

"She's not?"

"No. She met an old flame. And ignited."

"Oh. *She* met someone."

"Yes. Why did you come, Tory?"

"To tell you something."

"What?"

"Are you like this in the courtroom?"

"Yes. They still call me Bulldog Reed. What did you come to tell me?"

"I forget."

"No, you don't."

"Let me put it another way. If I remembered, I wouldn't tell you."

"I'll stay out here until you do."

"You will not."

"Yes, I will."

"Fine. Go ahead." She folded her arms over her chest. "Would you like a cookie?"

"Not if you made them."

"That's not a very nice thing to say to a woman you are trying to woo."

"Woo who? You? What makes you think that?"

"How about those flowers?"

"Just helping a couple of poor kids get to college."

"You love me madly," she said.

A little smile tugged at the corner of his lips.

"Is that what you came to tell me?" he asked.

"Yes, that you love me madly, and want to spend the rest of your life chasing me around the bedroom hoping for a chance to tickle my toes."

"That's what you came to tell me?"

"Nearly."

"Nearly?"

"Except," she took a deep and shaky breath, "for the word *you*, you can substitute *I*. I love you madly."

"Ah, Tory."

She snuck a glance at his handsome profile then looked back to her flowers trying to decipher what that meant. *Ah, Tory*. It could mean damn near anything. Her heart laid out at his feet and he chooses to be enigmatic.

"And when did you discover this?" he asked quietly,

after the silence had drawn out forever between them. "That you loved me madly?"

She took a deep breath. In for a penny, in for a pound. Why not tell him? Why not tell him everything?

She was being given a second chance. It was a choice between telling him the truth or trying to survive the rest of her life with the help of Maple Walnut ice cream and the soaps.

It might end up at that anyway.

But it might not.

She wished she at least looked good. She reached up and touched the head of a snapdragon that grew out of the nearest planter. She studied it intensely.

He did not speak, push her or rush her. He was not going to make this any easier for her.

"Forever," she croaked. "From the day I first met you."

Out of the corner of her eye, she saw he was not surprised, as she had thought he would be. He nodded slightly.

"You knew," she said softly.

"I guessed. Last night."

"How?"

"I don't know. It just came to me. And then I knew what Mark had always known. Why I stayed away.

"I loved you. Every time I looked at you, it would have been there in my eyes. That I loved you and that I couldn't stop. I would never have been able to pretend that it wasn't true. And so I left, and Mark knew I left so that you would never hurt over your choice, never ever wish you had made it differently. He knew I couldn't hurt you. Or him. Bless his soul, he saw that as my gift to him."

"It was your gift to him," she said quietly. "And to

me. You knew, sooner or later, I would turn from him and look at you and the whole world would have been able to see what was in my eyes. And when he was sick, and I felt so alone sometimes, I wanted you to come. And was so glad when you didn't.''

"You would have never betrayed him, Tory."

"You saw to that."

"It's not in you."

"I hope not. I'm glad you didn't put me to the test."

"Why did you marry Mark?" he asked.

She looked at the flowers and the deck Mark had built, and she remembered his quiet smile and his quiet way, and the way she had felt with him. Safe. Cherished.

"Because I loved him," she said softly.

Adam nodded. "It was not a mistake for you to marry him.''

The tears were running down her cheeks. "I know."

"It was exactly what was meant to be. You didn't marry the wrong man. If you ever tell any member of the bar I said this, I will deny it, but I think there is an order to the universe. And I believe when you married Mark, you obeyed it. You were given a sacred trust, sent to you from a different plane. From heaven, if you will. A love that had its place and time and would not and could not be denied.''

She nodded through the tears that were pouring down her eyes. Adam came to her, and just like that first morning, he lifted her onto his lap and caught her tears against his chest, and ran his fingers through her hair.

And talked to her. About love and how good it was. The only force really capable of changing the world for the better at all. How he didn't believe real love ever hurt, only healed.

About how strong her love for Mark had made her.

Better even than she had been before.

"And now it's our turn," Adam said, "to be together. To make the world a better place simply by loving one another."

She looked up at him. His face swam through the tears. "Are you asking me to marry you?"

"Yes."

"Oh, Adam, how can one woman be so honored? How can one woman have two men love her like this?"

"She would have to be a very special woman."

"But I'm not. I'm just ordinary."

"Ah, Tory."

"I don't know what *Ah, Tory* means!"

"It means you don't see about yourself what the rest of the world sees."

"Such as?"

"The love. That shines out of your eyes and your heart and touches everyone you touch. That love that you send out in these bundles of flowers, and that you have poured into your garden and your house. All around you is what you are, Tory. Beautiful."

"Don't say that when my hair looks like this."

"Beautiful," he repeated firmly.

"I don't want to live in Toronto," she said.

"Funny thing, neither do I."

"Where do you want to live?"

"Where do you?"

"You know that night when we went to Banff, and you talked about going around the world with just a few earthly possessions and a motorcycle?"

He laughed softly.

"That's what I want to do."

"You?"

"Adam, I have played it safe my whole life. I've repressed that side of me that wants to climb mountains and learn to surf. I want to ride wild horses, and learn to speak Spanish in Spain.''

He was looking down at her, laughing.

''Are you shocked?'' she asked him.

''No. I always knew that you wished it was you riding that bicycle over the cliff instead of me.''

''And why wasn't it?''

''You needed a push.''

''Are you going to push me?'' she asked.

''No,'' he said.

''You aren't?''

''No.''

''Why not?''

''Because Mark already did.''

It was true. In the strangest of ironies it was quiet and stable Mark who had taught her that life was short. To live it to the fullest would involve taking risks. There were no guarantees. There was no safe way.

Except to follow the path of one's own heart.

The doorbell rang, and when they ignored it, it rang again.

''It's probably Daniel,'' Adam said. ''He probably wants a tip.''

''Tell him to get an education,'' she suggested.

''I already did.''

''He told me you were going to get him a scholarship.''

''Yeah, well, I'll do what I can.''

''Adam, quit pretending you're not a nice guy.''

''You'll probably have to push me for me to stay that way.''

''No, I won't,'' she said with a smile. ''Mark already did.''

The doorbell rang again.

"He's persistent, anyway," Adam said, "and a really bright kid. I had a look at some of his transcripts when I returned the motorbike yesterday. For a guy who goes to school one day out of five, he has about an 82 percent average."

"Just like someone else we both knew and loved," she said dryly.

The doorbell rang again.

"I can't stand it," she said, and got up and went through her kitchen. She paused for a moment and looked at it carefully. At all her "stuff."

She wondered if she was going to miss it, and knew suddenly she would not. She could always replace it when the adventure was done.

As if, with Adam at her side, the adventure would ever be done.

The doorbell rang again, and she went to it and opened it.

It was not Daniel who stood there.

"I could barely get to your door for all the flowers," the man said with annoyance. He wore a three-piece suit, and his face was pinched and without humor.

Tory could not bring herself to apologize for the flowers. Her front porch was jam-packed full of them. The smell was heavenly.

"Help yourself to some for your wife," she suggested, opening the screen door and taking the envelope he offered her.

"No, thank you," he said primly. "Sign here."

She signed. The envelope was from a law firm she had never heard of. He turned and picked his way delicately through the flowers.

And suddenly, in him she saw what too much predictability could do. It could turn life sour. Wanting everything always to be safe and neat could drain the joy from life.

"Take some of the flowers," she called. "It might change your whole life."

He turned and looked at her, and seemed about to refuse again. And then it was as if he saw the blooms for the first time.

"These ones are kind of pretty," he said reluctantly, picking up a particularly passionate bouquet of blood-red roses.

She smiled.

He smiled back, tentatively, and sniffed the roses.

Well, maybe his whole life would not be changed, but his face was already improved.

She went back to Adam. "It wasn't Daniel. It's something from a law office. Here. You read it. I probably won't understand it anyway."

He took the letter. He recognized the name of the law firm on the return address. He opened it and read:

"As per our client, deceased, Mr. Mark Mitchell's request, the following document is being forwarded to you on this date."

He looked at Tory. She looked back at him, wide-eyed. "What is it?" she asked.

Behind the official looking letter typed on linen paper was a humble piece of blue-lined foolscap.

"It's a letter," he said, "from Mark."

"Read it."

"Dear Tory and Adam—"

"How did he know we'd be together?"

"I think he knew what was going to happen if he got us together."

"Read it!"

"I will if you quit interrupting."

"All right. All right."

"Dear Tory and Adam:
  Congratulations.

                                    Love, Mark."

"That's it?" Tory asked.

Adam turned the paper over, and nodded.

"There is no way he could have known you just asked me to marry you," Tory said.

"My legal mind says the very same thing. But my heart says he knew. He always knew. He's glad for us, Tory. That's what he wanted us to know."

"He really is watching out for us," she whispered in wonder. "Do you think he always will?"

"I think every single time we need a bicycle-drawn ricksha to show up or a motorcycle to break down, we'll know he's with us."

She laughed, and Adam laughed, and for one suspended and dazzling moment he was right there. Mark was laughing with them.

Tory looked at Adam and at the pure love shining in his face as he reread that brief note and then looked up at her. She felt something in her opening like a blossom that had waited for the sun. Out of the rich and deep soil of her sadness and heartbreak she could feel joy pushing through. Love would not be refused.

And love was always the final victor in life. Always.

"Adam," she said softly, "there is something I need from you."

As he watched her, she slipped off her socks, lifted her feet onto the patio table and wiggled her toes luxuriously. And then, shouting with laughter, with him in hot pursuit, she ran barefoot for the bedroom.

*   *   *   *   *

If you enjoyed what you just read,
then we've got an offer you can't resist!

Take 2 bestselling love stories FREE!

Plus get a FREE surprise gift!

Clip this page and mail it to Silhouette Reader Service™

IN U.S.A.	IN CANADA
3010 Walden Ave.	P.O. Box 609
P.O. Box 1867	Fort Erie, Ontario
Buffalo, N.Y. 14240-1867	L2A 5X3

YES! Please send me 2 free Silhouette Romance® novels and my free surprise gift. Then send me 6 brand-new novels every month, which I will receive months before they're available in stores. In the U.S.A., bill me at the bargain price of $2.90 plus 25¢ delivery per book and applicable sales tax, if any*. In Canada, bill me at the bargain price of $3.25 plus 25¢ delivery per book and applicable taxes**. That's the complete price and a savings of over 10% off the cover prices—what a great deal! I understand that accepting the 2 free books and gift places me under no obligation ever to buy any books. I can always return a shipment and cancel at any time. Even if I never buy another book from Silhouette, the 2 free books and gift are mine to keep forever. So why not take us up on our invitation. You'll be glad you did!

215 SEN CNE7
315 SEN CNE9

Name	(PLEASE PRINT)	
Address	Apt.#	
City	State/Prov.	Zip/Postal Code

* Terms and prices subject to change without notice. Sales tax applicable in N.Y.
** Canadian residents will be charged applicable provincial taxes and GST.
 All orders subject to approval. Offer limited to one per household.
 ® are registered trademarks of Harlequin Enterprises Limited.

SROM99   ©1998 Harlequin Enterprises Limited

This August 1999, the legend
continues in Jacobsville

DIANA PALMER

LOVE WITH A LONG, TALL TEXAN

A trio of brand-new short stories featuring
three irresistible Long, Tall Texans

GUY FENTON, LUKE CRAIG and CHRISTOPHER DEVERELL...

This August 1999, Silhouette brings readers an
extra-special collection for Diana Palmer's legions
of fans. Diana spins three unforgettable stories of
love—Texas-style! Featuring the men you can't get
enough of from the wonderful town of Jacobsville,
this collection is a treasure for all fans!

*They grow 'em tall in the saddle in Jacobsville—and
they're the best-looking, sweetest-talking men to be
found in the entire Lone Star state. They are proud,
hardworking men of steel and it will take
the perfect woman to melt their hearts!*

Don't miss this collection of original
Long, Tall Texans stories...available in
August 1999 at your favorite retail outlet.

SILHOUETTE BOOKS
is proud to announce the arrival of

THE BABY OF THE MONTH CLUB:

the latest installment of author
Marie Ferrarella's
popular miniseries.

When pregnant Juliette St. Claire met Gabriel Saldana than she discovered he wasn't the struggling artist he claimed to be. An undercover agent, Gabriel had been sent to Juliette's gallery to nab his prime suspect: Juliette herself. But when he discovered her innocence, would he win back Juliette's heart and convince her that he was the daddy her baby needed?

Don't miss Juliette's induction into
THE BABY OF THE MONTH CLUB
in September 1999.
Available at your favorite retail outlet.

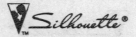